JAMAL MAHJOUB was born in London in 1960. His father is Sudanese and his mother English. He spent his early childhood in Liverpool before the family moved to the Sudan where he attended the Comboni College in Khartoum, a school run by Italian Catholic Priests.

Having completed his schooling, Mahjoub studied Geology at the University of Sheffield. He did not however pursue a career in Geology but worked instead in a variety of jobs ranging from fast food cooking and motorcycle despatch riding to telephone sales and finance marketing.

Mahjoub currently lives in Denmark with his wife who is expecting their first child. *Navigation of a Rainmaker* is his first novel.

JAMAL MAHJOUB

NAVIGATION OF A RAINMAKER

HEINEMANN

Heinemann International
a division of Heinemann Educational Books Ltd
Halley Court, Jordan Hill, Oxford OX2 8EJ

Heinemann Educational Books Inc
70 Court Street, Portsmouth, New Hampshire, 03801, USA

Heinemann Educational Books (Nigeria) Ltd
PMB 5205, Ibadan
Heinemann Kenya Ltd
Kijabe Street, PO Box 45314, Nairobi
Heinemann Educational Boleswa
PO Box 10103, Village Post Office, Gaborone, Botswana
Heinemann Educational Books (Caribbean) Ltd
175 Mountain View Avenue, Kingston 6, Jamaica

LONDON   EDINBURGH   MELBOURNE
SYDNEY   AUCKLAND   SINGAPORE   MADRID

First published by Heinemann International
in the African Writers Series in 1989

British Library Cataloguing in Publication Data

Mahjoub, Jamal
    Navigation of a rainmaker. – (African writers
    series).
    I. Title   II. Series
    823 [F]
    ISBN 0–435–90560–0

Phototypeset by Wilmaset, Birkenhead, Wirral
Printed in Great Britain by
Cox and Wyman, Reading, Berkshire

. . . the bad food, unhealthy houses, insufficient clothing, problems of all kinds, boredom, a continual rage against niggers as stupid as they are crooked. One year here is the same as five someplace else; you get old quickly here like all the rest of the Sudan.

ARTHUR RIMBAUD

(In a letter to his mother, dated 20 February 1891)

NORTH

ONE

In a place such as this: where the wind turns on silent stone, where, if you pause for a moment in that instant of turmoil when the dawn sweeps the cold night back into the stagnant stars, you can smell the emptiness that lingers here. It waits for the sullen heat of day to arrive. Gently the sun comes creeping over the edge of the blue earth. The horizon is a line of red slashed into the cobalt sky, still sad and hollow from the night before. The elusive stars vanish slowly into the monochromatic semi-arc of a halo that announces the sun. As it steals into the melting blue, so the light changes: burning from red to a furious incandescent white. So the silent dawn air is replaced once again by a layer of pure heat that hangs over the sand like a blanket.

The old man watched the sun rise, just as he did every morning. He enjoyed being alone at this time of day, finding comfort in the habit just as he found peace in the solitude. Today, though, he found himself praying that nature would not follow its course, hoping that somehow the habit could be broken. As he looked down from the low outcrop the desert began to come to life; the sand began to shimmer and shift in its tracks and the wind hummed through the thorn bushes, making them rustle with delight.

The desert is a broken place where the wind and the sand and the stars live. Anything else is no longer welcome. The desert has seasons just like any other part of the world. Further to the west of the place where the old man watched the day beginning, the rains had come and turned the land green and the ground would soon be dotted with bush and wild trees. The wells would fill with water so that everyone could drink their fill; life could go on. The old man had seen drought before. In his sixty years of nomadic life he had seen waterholes dry up like a bone, waterholes that people swore would never dry out and which no one could remember having dried out before. The desert was full of surprises; the rains pleased themselves. Some years it didn't please them to come and who could argue with that? Perhaps only Allah. The old man

3

knew this land, he understood the way it breathed. He could feel the steady beat of its heart through the soles of his feet worn hard by the rocks and the sand. He and his family were on their way south and in all his life he had never seen so many abandoned camps; the whole country was on the move. The rains were very late – even the deepest holes had run dry. It had been a big mistake to be caught this far north. The old man knew that they would have to travel as fast as they could to the more populated areas, to the water pipes and the towns.

Picking up his wooden staff polished smooth by years of use, the old man turned away from the sunrise towards the camp. There were already signs of movement from the damar – smoke was beginning to rise in curling wraiths from a small fire. He started down the rocky ground towards the shelter. His leather sandals slapped against his hard feet, his legs – frail-looking but sinewy and strong like coiled springs – bending with the movement.

The tents were set facing east in the hard, gravel-covered ground. The old man went to each of the three tents in turn and called out to the occupants while standing in the doorway with his back to the entrance. They were his family, all these people: his wife and children, her sister and her husband, their children. When he'd roused them he went back to join his brother-in-law who stood by the fire fanning the flames with a piece of cardboard.

The procession got under way with the usual bustle of activity, though every day, thought the old man, it seemed to take longer. They were tired, all of them. Finally the march started. The old man walked at the front, leading the first camel which carried his wife and her belongings. They were heading south and east on a path which they rarely used. Each well they had come to was dry. Everyone they met told the same story. The land was drying up, shrivelling like a leaf in front of their eyes. They carried on from one place to the next, but it was always the same story.

The old man and his family stopped at midday. The camels could go for maybe ten days without water but there was no point in exhausting them by driving them too hard. There was a good chance, with this continued hard walking, that they would go lame. The travellers couldn't stop for a day, and they couldn't afford one of the animals going lame. That was the last thing they wanted now. They constructed a shelter and sat down to rest a little before the cool of late afternoon when, said the old man, they would do another hour's walking before stopping for the night.

He leaned back with his head on his arm and closed his eyes. Just then a

4

Mig jet roared low overhead, the screech of the jet engines jolting him awake. In an instant the camp was filled with the excited chatter of the children as they pointed at the black dot disappearing into the sun.

Behind them a dust-storm began to gather.

TWO

Sand, sand was everywhere. There was nothing, and then there was sand. His body was totally buried in a layer of living, breathing, moving sand. This was not ordinary sand – this sand had a mind of its own, a mind and a soul, a sense of character, a presence. It was a surprise; he was not sure how long he had been caught up like this. He realised that he was losing his orientation; all perception of space and confinement of space was vanishing. He could not see in front of him. He stumbled, unable to place his feet. Time and space had deserted him. He had no idea where the ground started and the sky left off. His arms waved uselessly. The wind tore at his clothes, flinging the sand at his face, stinging the skin until it felt raw. The tiny grains formed a continuous stream that worked away at the exposed surface of his unprotected hands and his face. Like stones in a river bed, they were being worn smooth by the flow. These lines on his hands and fingers – lines of fate, life lines: the marks of his individual existence were being erased for ever. The scratches and the small scars picked up along the way, marks where the flesh had grown over to heal wounds left by the earth's touch: all were being obliterated. Surely they were all that was left, the only evidence that this vapour soul had in fact passed across the face of life.

The sand clogged his throat and stung his eyes, drawing tears. He tried to concentrate his thoughts but his mind was drowning. He was here for a reason, but even the fleeting essence of reason had vanished. He was stumbling now, trying to stand. His feet were buried in a moving, living blanket of coarse brown dust. He staggered, almost falling. The sweat formed a film of grime over his body and face. Direction had no meaning, so where was he going?

6

Exhaustion pulled his legs down while the wind howled around his head and tailless eddies whirled him through this timeless spin. Abandoned by reason, he searched for reason where it could not exist. Without direction, how could there be reason? Without warning, his knees buckled and he found himself sinking down. Pulling himself up, he stumbled on, his feet finding support only at the very last instant. The sand seemed to draw itself in around his shoulders, embracing him like a shawl. He moved two, three paces, and he began to count slowly. The paces became shorter, and the numbers ticked by like so many forgotten years. He could no longer clear his throat from the suffocating dust; it was getting harder to breathe. He found himself again on his knees. How many times was that? His mind was clouding, slipping from his weakening grasp. The sand weaved about him like a demented wraith, and he sank slowly. His heart's pulses reached a deafening crescendo before finally wrenching free. The lifeless body dissolved. The cloud of dust rained down grain after grain and gradually there was no more. He was no more.

The air-conditioner rumbled outside the window. Every few minutes the noise would change its tone, becoming a slower flapping sound as the belt began to slip on the motor wheel. It ground slowly down until the engine was almost silent, then at the last moment it would burst back into life as the belt jumped back into place.

Tanner's eyes opened as the machine shuddered into life. For a second he thought that it was still night. His eyes adjusted to the gloom and he saw that a thin cold glimmer of dawn was beginning to touch the wooden shutters of the window. His body felt clammy against the sheets and he realised that he must have been sweating. He pressed the thin sheet against his body to dry it. He felt weary. Without moving, he lay on his back and stared at the ceiling, listening to the rumble of the air-conditioner.

He knew he must have been dreaming, from the lingering aftertaste. He couldn't remember what he had dreamt about, but it left him with a sense of loss as though he had heard news of a death – someone close to him, a friend or a close relative. His mouth was dry so he got up from the bed and wandered naked out of the room on to the veranda. The water was ice cold, sinking through his body like a knife, too swiftly past the dry throat, too heavily on the stomach. He closed the refrigerator door and went back to his room. He lay back on his bed in the dark and reached out with his hand for the cigarettes he'd left on the bedside table. He found one and lit it, exhaled and punched the button on the tape player. Miles Davis filled the room with 'Moon Dreams'. Tanner watched the light creeping up the slats of the wooden shutters, throwing patterns on the wall.

Outside the noise from the street said that the quiet lower-middle class of white-collar suburbia was coming awake. He savoured this quiet moment, awake and alone. Somehow the world had not quite intruded into the space between the tiny death of sleep and the birth of the new day. There was a moment here which carried with it a feeling that was almost, but not quite, power over destiny, and in the same moment utter despair. He tried to remember the dream he had last night, but drowning was the only word that came to mind. Finally he gave up as it was surely out of reach; if his memory had erased it then perhaps he didn't need it. Maybe it would come back to him some time. People did that, he'd read it somewhere: remember things that they'd forgotten years ago.

He got out of bed and dressed quickly in a loose cotton shirt and dark trousers. Slipping on a pair of battered leather sandals, he went to find some breakfast. He crossed the veranda of fading and cracked tiles that once were red but now were a dull maroon, and stepped out from the shelter into the open yard that separated the main house from the single room that was the kitchen. The hard baked earth that covered the yard was still cool and dark from the night. The sunlight was creeping slowly in between the shadows of the walls.

The screen door squeaked and swayed on its ancient hinges. He fried some eggs in a layer of cottonseed oil. The oil had an overpowering aroma that almost obliterated the taste of the eggs themselves, but it was the only thing available in the *souk* at the moment. These things went in phases – if it wasn't one thing it would be another. He ate the eggs from the frying-pan with some stale bread that he'd bought days ago.

It was a Friday, which meant that all the offices in town would be closed. Not that he was seriously thinking about going into the office, though really, he thought to himself, it was about time that he did. He had been given a week off after they'd got back from the Red Sea. That was three weeks ago exactly. They were probably wondering where he'd got himself to, but then again they probably weren't all that bothered. They couldn't phone him – the phone had been out of order for months. In fact he couldn't remember the last time the phone had worked.

From across the high wall at the back of the house came the sound of a small child crying. Tanner walked back across the yard to the house. In the short space of time he'd spent in the kitchen, the sun had filled the yard completely. The ground was already building up towards the blistering heat of midday. The only trace of shadow was a narrow strip that ran across from the side wall of the house, the only reminder of the cool that the night had brought. A scrawny tabby cat with one bad eye slipped along this strip in search of scraps.

Tanner went back into his air-cooled room and left the shutters closed. He sat on the unmade bed and lit another cigarette. He picked up the paper, a copy of *Newsweek* that was almost a month old. He couldn't remember how many times he'd read the same stories over again. It was almost a ritual now. He knew there was nothing new in it, but nevertheless he had nothing else to read. It was hard to get hold of papers here. Most were imported and therefore out of date when they arrived, as well as being sold at extortionate prices. All the other papers sold in Khartoum were in Arabic, which he couldn't read. While he went through *Newsweek* again, he listened to the air-conditioner rumbling away unevenly and wondered why it didn't just give up.

His room was not big. The bed was placed in the centre so as to be in the direct path of the air duct. There was a mahogany wardrobe in one corner, its panels cracked and battered; on the outside of one of its doors a long mirror was precariously hung.

There were two tables: a small bedside one with a lamp on it, and a larger one, covered in maps and books, in the opposite corner to the wardrobe, next to the window that never seemed to be open. Water seeped from a pipe that ran through the wall, causing the paint to form into blisters that eventually cracked, leaving gaping holes in the paintwork where the sandy-coloured plaster underneath peered through.

A yellow-green salamander about six inches long paused halfway up the wall, staring through unblinking eyes, frozen momentarily before scurrying behind a picture that hung there.

Over the uneven rumble of the air-cooler, the sound of a street pedlar came in from the baking hot road outside.

'*Angareeb!*' A rope man to fix the beds, chanting as he moved on down the street. Tanner relaxed and leaned back on the bed that was dry and cool now. Glancing round the four walls, he thought back to the six weeks he'd spent out in the field: enduring the noise and continual vibration of the Land Rover, coming back at night to dusty bedrolls and hard floors. All of that seemed a long way off. He couldn't tell whether it was a good or bad thing to be back here. The relief at having arrived back to comparative luxury and rest was mixed with a discomfort that bordered on revulsion for this place.

He lay back and pushed the rest of the world out of his mind, listening to the cool dark of the room. Safe within these dusty walls, he hid beneath the noisy rattle of the air-cooler and soon fell asleep.

Tanner dozed on and off for most of the day. At one point he tried writing a letter to his father but he failed to get any further than the first line: 'Hope this finds you in good health . . .' He wrote to his father from time to time, every six months or so, but he had never had a reply. Nevertheless he felt the need to describe what he had found here, and especially to his father.

When Tanner woke again, it was dusk. He came away slowly, like a man who has no real wish to return to the world. He lay there clinging to the sense of drift that comes with sleep, but the dream state left him. It slipped away, leaving him with a longing for something he could not quite put his finger on. The world around him was utterly silent, as if everything had stopped moving. He listened, but there wasn't a breath of sound, not a murmur.

The lights had gone again and the room was pitch black. He stumbled outside into the yard and stretched against the night sky.

Tanner was hungry now. He went to the kitchen to collect an enamelled metal dish and went out into the street. The power cut meant that the street was lit only by the stars and the moon. Down the road a car came slowly, picking its way through the unmarked potholes, almost coming to a standstill at the unavoidable ones. The headlights picked out the heaps of dust and garbage that lined the narrow street. The beam fell on Tanner as he walked along; he stepped out of the light on to the remains of broken pavement. The car rolled quietly past.

He reached the small corner shop which was in essence a converted garage: a single room with a battered wooden counter tacked in place across the mouth. The counter was made from dismantled packing cases held together with hastily nailed strips of aluminium and tin hammered out of jerrycans. The whole room was lit by a single gloomy hurricane lamp. It smelled of carbolic soap and tobacco. The man behind the counter was a thin cross-eyed character with scars high on each cheek. He wore loose-fitting pants and a long shirt that stretched as far as his knees. With a lopsided grin that could have been taken for a sneer, the man took Tanner's money and tucked it into the gaudy biscuit tin that acted as a cash register. Wiping his hands on the filthy cotton outfit he wore, the man took Tanner's dish and scooped into it a ladle of hot beans from a globe-shaped cauldron.

Taking the dish, Tanner walked back along the uneven road to the house. The lights were still off and the house was dark and empty. The small garden rustled with the soft wind that blew through the two neglected lime trees growing there. Tanner crossed the garden round to the yard at the back, collecting a plastic chair from the veranda as he went by. He ate with his fingers, using the bread that he'd brought to lift the dark beans to his mouth. He ate in a silence that was broken only by the occasional bark of a stray dog somewhere, or the odd voice that

11

drifted over the wall from the next-door house. These particular neighbours were often quite noisy, being a large family with an inordinate number of screaming children. The house frequently resonated with the clamour of excited voices – which made this quiet evening all the more unusual.

Tanner ate slowly. When he had finished, he lit a cigarette and watched the silent lights of a jet airliner float gently across the open sky beneath the scatter of diamond pinprick stars. Outside in the street a stray dog howled.

It was well past midnight, nearly two hours after curfew time, when Tanner left the house. The streets were deserted. Far away the sound of a lone car was carried on the wind. He paused to hear which way it was going, and the noise vanished into the shadows. From his house he walked down towards the bottom end of the area he lived in. It was relatively new, this part, the houses built as an extension to the older sections of the town.

Tanner reached the edge of the extension and looked both ways. While the police in general were not over-diligent about the curfew, they were still enforcing it.

The road was a narrow two-lane strip of tarmac that kept close to the edge of the painted brick walls and metal railings with their decorative wrought-iron birds and flowers. On the other side, between the tarmac and the adobe walls of another block of houses beyond, was a strip of dirt about six times the width of the hard road. It was criss-crossed with tyre tracks and quiet now like fossil traces of some kind of animal that only emerged in daylight. The strip looked clear, so Tanner stepped away from the wall where he was standing and began to cross. He reached the other side and ducked down a narrow street. He knew where he was going and fifteen minutes later turned a corner and reached a narrow doorway. He tapped on the tall green metal gate and it opened immediately.

Caesar the pimp looked out, a short man with a gold tooth that glinted in the gleam from the flashlight which he shone in Tanner's face to identify him. Nodding in recognition, he held the door open, glancing furtively out before he shut and bolted it behind him. Tanner followed Caesar down a long passageway between the walls of two houses, the flashlight beam jumping around back and forth ahead of them, pointing out a step here or a dip in the ground there. The passageway led through to an inner courtyard, which in turn gave on to a number of small house units. Caesar knocked on one of the doors. It opened after a moment's pause and light from within the room flooded out, illuminating the two men who stood in the shadows. Tanner stepped inside, handing a roll of crumpled notes to Caesar as he passed him. The gold tooth glinted in reply.

The girl who waited for him inside was the same girl he had seen the last time and the time before. He had come to prefer her. He had thought at first that it made little difference, but had come to realise that this wasn't true: he had his preferences like anyone else. She wasn't particularly pretty, but he was drawn by the melancholy he saw in her.

She laughed when she saw him, a long jarring laugh. On the table was a bottle of *aaraqui*, the pure spirit alcohol made from fermented dates which smelt like petrol and tasted much the same. He broke the seal on the top and poured two glasses.

The room was cramped, although it was not a small room in itself. The walls were hung with rugs and paintings and wood carvings, many of erotic scenes, while the floor was piled with wool carpets and soft cushions.

The room was lit by two hurricane lamps, the glass windows of which had been painted with a garish red colour. Tanner finished his drink and helped himself to another one. The girl, whose name Tanner was sure he knew but could not remember at the moment, put her glass down on the small table. She went over to the wide high bed and sat on the edge of the rough wooden frame. The zipper on the side of her cheap dress was made in Hong Kong and would not come free at first. When she had undressed, Tanner stubbed out his cigarette and moved over to join her. Neither of them said a word.

The lamps went out and the moon glow blew through the bars of the narrow window high on the wall above the bed.

13

It took him three days to hitch there. When he got to the outskirts of Aberdeen the snow was falling thick and fast. The motorway was lined with helpless vehicles broken down, lying askew, stranded in disbelief.

The last ride he got was in a big removals van taking office furniture into the city.

'Going the wrong way, aren't you, lad? In this bloody weather?'

The driver wore a baseball cap that read 'Dallas Cowboys'. He called himself the 'Buxton Cowboy' on the CB which he fiddled with constantly. Under the cap he wore pink earmuffs to keep his head warm and protected from the icy blast that blew through the open window.

The slipways were lined with figures huddled in the grey light, thumbs outstretched. All at the start of a mythical journey south to a new life, a new beginning. Bowed forwards against the wind, they shuffled about to keep warm.

'They're all heading south – no one comes to Aberdeen this time of year, nothing here for them, you see.'

It was dark when they got to the centre of the town. Tanner thanked the driver who rolled off somewhere else. He wandered through the granite city until eventually he found a room for the night.

Tanner spent the next day asking directions to another rooming house, one which he had the address for already.

It didn't take him long to find what he was looking for. Across the street from the row of houses was a collection of small shops. Having realised that his confidence had been swept away in the icy gusting wind, he crossed into a small steamed-up café. He bought himself a mug of tea and went to sit in the window. People came and went in a familiar sort of way between the fried breakfasts and the disgruntled conversation. Tanner picked up a discarded newspaper that was lying on a nearby table. He began to read, keeping one eye on the window. After a time he fished the crumpled photograph out of his pocket and surveyed the now familiar portrait once again. The man in the picture was small in build. His complexion seemed darker than Tanner's, but this might have been the harsh lighting of a studio. His hair was parted across one side as though it had been applied cosmetically. It seemed at odds with the tight curls and the pattern of scars cut into each cheek. The conflict of the hairstyle and the tribal scars seemed to combine into the confusion that tinged the deeply receded eyes staring straight through the camera. Tanner put the picture away in his pocket and cleared a gap in the misted window to look across the street again. The photograph was taken perhaps thirty years ago but it was the most consistent memory that he had of his father's appearance. He wondered if he had changed much in the ten years since he saw him last.

He didn't have much time to think about the question because at that moment a door across the road opened inwards and an old man emerged. He was huddled inside a donkey jacket that looked a couple of sizes too large for him and he carried a stick with which he tested the ground for a moment or two before venturing out.

Tanner sprang to his feet, knocking over the chair in his confusion. He didn't notice the funny looks as he made for the door. Pulling on his coat, he crossed the street and fell into step a few paces behind the man who was his father. It was beginning to snow again. Large splayed-out flakes floated on the wind to drop like dust in his hair. They stood together at the bus stop, Tanner not daring to step forward and speak. He spent the whole day following him round town. They went through the shopping precinct and waited in the Unemployment Office. They even went to a pub where the old man sat in a corner with a bottle of brown ale and read a newspaper. It was dark by the time they were back and Tanner dutifully followed all the way until he turned into the house.

The following day Tanner returned to the café to sit and continue his vigil. He had spent the night freezing on a park bench, cursing himself for not having the nerve to open his mouth. He asked himself what it was that he had come here expecting. He surprised himself with the question. There had been no doubt in his mind that he must try at least to reach his father before he left the country, possibly for good.

The idea of travelling to the Sudan had grown in his mind over the last year or so. It began to occupy that part of him which had always been empty. The idea grew to encompass everything that seemed to be lacking from his life. Listless, he now had direction. Dejected, he now discovered hope. There was one prerequisite: if he was to return to the land of his origin (and indeed he did see it as a journey back to some point of divergence) then he must first contact the one man who might tell him what he could expect to find once he arrived there.

The last time he had seen his father was on one of his rare visits after the divorce. He had not come down at all since Tanner's mother had remarried. He must have been around fourteen the last time they had met. At that time he had not wanted to encourage their relationship. He was so much younger then. Now he recognised all too well the regret he felt. It was time to redress the balance if it wasn't too late.

The café was warm and pleasant enough but he felt the thread of time dragging him to the door every time a customer walked out. The weather looked like it was clearing at last and perhaps he saw this as a sign. Either way, he had waited long enough. He found himself standing up and making for the door to the street. He crossed over and approached the small gate, pushing it open. There was a sign in the window that said 'No Vacancies' and he walked up to the door and pressed the bell.

The hallway was narrow and constricted. There was a table by the stairs, a mirror over the table. The striped wallpaper was brightly decorated with alternating pink and jade green. There was a telephone with a coin-box and a biro on a piece of string just inside the front door. A coatstand with a donkey jacket.

The door to the other room was slightly open. He could hear the murmur of voices and glimpse the low light from inside. The door opened and she appeared again. Silently she smiled and beckoned him to the door, standing aside to let him in. The room was smaller than he'd imagined, with thick carpets and low lights. There was a table by the window where the curtains were drawn against the street. There was a small sofa and an armchair. Against one side was a set of shelves with glass ornaments and a

16

porcelain bowl decorated with sunflowers, a bottle of Campari and a silver candelabra. The television was on, filling the room with Fred Flintstone.

The man in the armchair was bent forward with his hands resting on the arms of the chair. He appeared not to have noticed Tanner coming in. There was a movement behind him and Tanner turned to see the door closing the last few inches behind the woman. When he turned round he found the man looking straight at him. He felt as though they were strangers. He didn't know whether he should go over and shake hands or embrace him, perhaps, so he stood where he was without moving.

'Sit down, please.' The older man indicated the sofa next to him. Tanner sat down. The sofa was too soft and he sank into it, which made him feel ill at ease. He leaned forward resting his elbows on his knees.

'I thought I'd pay you a visit. Since I was in the area anyway, I thought I might as well come round.'

The man nodded.

'I thought I'd come over and see you before I go.' He paused because he wasn't sure his father was following. He wanted to be sure that he was understood.

'I'm going back.' He felt unsure suddenly, out of his depth. As if he were considering things for the first time: whether to go or not. What he was saying sounded irrational. He tried to smile. 'Back to the Sudan.'

'Of course, but you've been there before.'

'No, no, I've never been there.'

The old man was smiling the way people do when they don't quite understand what is going on. The television was making a lot of noise. Tanner found it hard to focus himself.

'Your mother never wanted to go there.'

'No, I know that.'

'She is a good woman though.'

'Yes.' Tanner realised they were talking at cross purposes.

'She takes care of me.' He leaned over and reached a finger across the space between them. 'You should not think badly of her.

17

She has taken care of me all these years.' He sat back as though considering the truth of his own words, nodding to himself slowly.

'I've always had the idea that, somehow, I would one day. Now seems like the right time.'

'I can't.'

'Can't what?' asked Tanner.

'I can't go with you.' He waved a hand in the air to indicate the room they were in. 'This is where I live,' he explained. 'I can't leave.'

'No.'

'That's why you came to see me, isn't it?' He was leaning across again, his brow furrowed. 'You wanted to take me back, didn't you?' He slumped back in the chair and clamped his eyes back on the television set. 'Well, I'm not going. I'm staying right here.'

'I didn't come here to take you with me. I just wanted to talk to you about it.' There was no sign of response. 'I thought you'd be happy, thought you'd want to wish me luck.' Still no change, not even a turn of the head. 'I don't know anyone there, I don't even know why I'm going. I just feel that I need to.' He hestitated, but he knew he would have to say it no matter how hollow it sounded. It was what he believed.

'I feel that part of me belongs there.'

The head turned and the eyes were torn finally from the flickering screen.

'I give you some advice, okay?' The finger pointed again. 'Forget about that part of you. You don't need it. You forget about it and sooner or later you'll realise that you don't need it.'

'I want to go.'

His father shrugged his shoulders.

The door opened and the woman came in. She smiled at Tanner and went over to the television set and switched it off. There was no change in the old man's expression.

'It's time for his tea,' she explained. 'Will you stay for something?'

'No,' said Tanner. 'I think I'd better get going.'

'Suit yourself,' she said and left the room. She had forgotten to

18

close the door behind her and it stood open like an unfinished sentence.

'I have to be off now,' he said. He felt there should have been more. He had expected something different. How could he have not guessed that he would be unwelcome? He held out his hand and gripped his father's thin spiny fingers in his.

She was waiting in the hallway. When he had closed the door behind him, she said, 'I couldn't help overhearing what you told him.' She tilted her head to one side. 'He's getting old, you know. It's difficult for him.' She paused. 'Anyway, maybe you'll find these useful.'

She handed him a map of the country where he was going and an address, torn from the flap of an envelope. He couldn't read the script.

'It's a friend, who might be able to help you over there,' she explained, tapping the paper.

'And this?' he asked, holding the old map up.

'Oh, it's an old survey map that I bought once in an antique shop. I thought it might look nice on the wall, but he didn't like it. You may as well have it.'

He took the map. What else was he to do?

THREE

On Monday morning Tanner woke up and knew instantly that it was time to go into the office. He had put the task off for long enough. More than anything else he was growing increasingly tired of his own company. He was tired of not knowing. Now that the decision was made there seemed to be no need to rush. He took his time getting ready, dressed and finished off his tea. He'd been in this state of withdrawal for nearly four weeks now so another ten minutes or so would make no difference. He was aware of a need to take his time.

The car he had was an old Fiat which the company had reluctantly lent him. It had once been blue but the sun had faded the paintwork in broad patches through to the bare metal underneath.

The sun was already making itself felt; though it was not yet nine o'clock the car was hot to touch. By midday it would be hot enough to fry an egg on the bonnet. The car started, though not without difficulty. The engine rattled and misfired. The car was badly kept as well as old.

The streets were full of holes, jagged scars ripped across the tarmac. Ten years ago these were new roads, but now they were little more than the bumpy dust tracks that lay beneath them. There were wider sections where the road had collapsed into the underground sewer system. Once Tanner had seen a whole car swallowed up by the road, headfirst with only the rear bumper protruding. In another ten years there would be nothing left of the roads. They'd given up repairing them. There had been a plea from the government some time ago that anyone who saw a hole in the road should attempt to repair it as best they could with what materials were available: bricks and sand, for example. But there

20

were still huge sections that had to be skirted round because they were impassable. Soon the tarmac would be ground away and it would all go back to where it had started; the roads would vanish into the dust, sucked back into the desert from where they had come.

The main road was a chaotic rush of movement and noise, sound and colour, like a heat-haze mirage that jumped and danced across the sand. Motor cars, ancient yellow taxis that rattled and choked in the dust and exhaust, music blaring through the open window from a radio. Dashboards covered in hanging prayer beads and lucky charms. Huge whale-shaped buses that were so overloaded they hung to one side, tailboards scraping the ground, threatening to keel over as they went round a corner. Prayers and painted inscriptions decorated the sides. People clung to each other in the doorways, dressed in billowing white cotton, hanging on with one arm like trapeze artists. The dust swirled in clouds round the lurching vehicles as they slowed down to receive even more passengers. No one seemed to get off – it would be impossible to get through the doorway. Men ran, clutching the hems of their long white *djellabias*, and leapt for the handrail as the bus careered off in a splutter of black diesel exhaust.

Everyone was going into town for some reason. They were going to the market or the office or to wander along the hot pavements and gaze at the shop windows. Maybe they were going to visit a relative who worked for the government, or to borrow money or pay off a loan from a friend, or to see a sick cousin in hospital or maybe to see the doctor themselves.

The bus he was behind bounced across the railway lines and swung past the main hospital, a sorry-looking building just down from the railway station. Its whitewashed walls were faded yellow by the sun and streaked with brown rust from last year's rains. The wards were overrun with wild cats that roamed the corridors at night. No one seemed able to do anything about it, or else nobody bothered.

People stood around in the street under the shade of a tree or a wall. Some were dressed in loose cotton shirts and trousers, western town clothes; others just wore the traditional one-piece

21

djellabia. They all stood and watched as the scene unfolded before them. This was their daily entertainment, a lifetime's vocation. Women and children, long trailing families, trudged through the dust by the road, oblivious to the chaos that rushed by them so close. Women no older than children themselves carried babies cradled on their hips. With their ragged hair and tattered clothes, they didn't use the buses unless they really had to. Three fine women dressed in bright clothes and golden jewellery stood under a large dusty tree, sweating with restraint into ornamental handkerchiefs, waiting for a taxi.

As he got closer to the centre, he felt the town begin to close in on him. He drove down the main road that led towards the presidential palace and the river. Here the roads were somewhat better off. Tanner turned away off El Qasr Avenue and drove past the sports stadium and the girls' school. The houses here were separated from the road and from each other by long hedgerows of tamarind. It was outside one of these houses, on a nondescript quiet side street, that Tanner parked the Fiat alongside a jeep on the strip of dust that was the pavement. Leaving the car open, he walked through the gate and up the gravel path.

The whole house belonged to Sutrol; it was their head office in Khartoum. As Tanner crossed the veranda past the open windows he could hear the rumble of an air-cooler and the stammer of a typewriter. In the sunlit garden a sprinkler hissed out jets of water that painted rainbows over the glistening lawn.

The reception desk was deserted and the phone ringing as Tanner crossed the hall and took the stairs to the first floor. Opposite the top of the stairs was a closed door with a plastic nameplate reading 'General Manager'. Tanner moved down the hall and ducked through an open doorway which led to the main office.

His desk was a large table, set into a corner, which he shared with three others. He realised it was nearly ten o'clock and everyone was out for breakfast, except the typist girl who never spoke to anyone and now sat in a corner fiddling with a sandwich, and one person working at the table, Suliman. He was an

22

industrious but unpopular character, who had been out in the field only once and had complained so much that since then everyone had refused to go on a trip that involved him, which suited Suliman fine. He looked up now as Tanner approached the desk. Pushing his glasses back up his nose, Suliman nodded in greeting and took the biro out of his mouth.

'You're still working here?' he asked quizzically.

'You didn't think I'd leave you to run this place all on your own, did you?' replied Tanner, sitting down at the desk.

Suliman let the joke pass without the hint of a smile. He went back to his papers, speaking without raising his head.

'We thought they left you out there with the vultures.'

Tanner looked round his desk. There were charts and maps he'd been given to study before the last trip. He folded them and pushed them into a drawer. He didn't want to think about the Red Sea Hills. There were reports that needed doing, field notes that needed writing out, samples to be analysed. There was plenty to do. Tanner looked across to where Suliman was scribbling furiously. Far away a phone rang and a typewriter clicked; they both stopped simultaneously. Tanner lit a cigarette and began to go through the desk, looking in all the drawers. He shuffled a hand through the loose papers and caught a splinter in his finger. He squeezed it and a drop of blood appeared. His mind turned to the dead girl.

She had been a student from the university, keen to get as much field experience as she could. It was strange for a girl to be doing something like geology in a country like this; even in this day and age the parameters of Islam meant that she was breaking laws, perhaps unwritten, about the behaviour of a woman. Not being a geologist himself, Tanner had no idea if she was at all competent, but he had drawn the conclusion after a month on the road that she was a forceful and determined person in any case. This was despite the fact that she rarely entered into light conversation. The other geologists, who were all men, seemed daunted by her, maybe even scared of her. She had died when the axle went on one of the trucks and it rolled over. By strange coincidence she was the only one killed. There were a couple of fractures and some bad cuts and bruises, but she was the only one who died.

'Can I see you in my office, Tanner, please.'

Tanner came back to the present to find Geoffrey Thompson, the general manager, standing in the doorway.

In his fifties, Thompson was a heavily built man who had been running the office for almost a year now. Tanner followed him down the hall to his small dark office opposite the stairs. He waited until Thompson had arranged himself behind the big desk that filled the room almost by itself.

'How many weeks have you been back now?' Thompson was fiddling with a report, trying to find a date, some kind of reference point. Tanner felt like he was a child again, a schoolboy summoned by the headmaster.

'Three weeks, I believe.'

'More like four,' replied Thompson.

Tanner stared past Thompson's shoulder at the map that covered most of the wall.

'There was nothing I could do about it. Those trucks should never have been used if they weren't safe.'

'We were assured the trucks had been checked. This was a major fault – this wasn't a flat battery or a faulty spark plug, the bloody axle snapped in half.'

'Something like that,' nodded Tanner.

Thompson pushed a hand through his thinning hair, shaking his head silently.

'She didn't come from a wealthy family – her father's a clerk somewhere in the Post Office, I think – so hopefully it won't create too much of a stink.'

Tanner nodded again. He really didn't want to discuss the matter. He was running out of patience. The map on the wall caught his eye again.

'But, dammit, where have you been? Four weeks since you got back and you haven't set foot in this office. You didn't even give me a report about her.'

'Hector was in charge of the expedition, he had all the details. Didn't you get his report?'

'I got his report,' said Thompson with obvious patience. 'But I would have liked an account from you as well. That is what you get paid for, isn't it?'

Tanner nodded yet again.

'I will give you my report. I just needed time to think about the whole business.'

Thompson leaned forward in his big leather chair, the stream of air from the air vent blowing the thin strands of his hair away from the widening bald patch on his head.

'She was highly recommended – the chancellor of the university came to see me himself. Do you know how many unemployed graduates there are in this town? Ten thousand! Ten thousand unemployed university graduates. She was one of the lucky ones because we let her go on the trip for some experience.'

He shrugged and looked at Tanner. What more was there to say?

Staring at the map on the wall, Tanner thought how odd the shape of the country was. It must be about twelve hundred miles from one end to the other. All covered in thin lines of various colours: green for roads, red lines for another kind or road, blue for rivers. There were also boundary lines that divided the map into provinces; they made little sense, much like the border lines that were supposed to cut one chunk of land away from the rest of Africa. The lines of greed and complete ignorance. Under colonial flags hammered out in blood and the death of so many who were lost and buried in the sand. The map of the Sudan looked like a face, the face of a man gazing down; the face of a man in mourning. The wars were carried on; tyrants come in all shapes and colours of the skin. So much hatred buried together – not even this country was big enough to hide them all. There was a corner in the top left-hand section of the map, the north west of the country. The space filled almost a quarter of the map. A quarter that was nothing but desert, a plateau of open empty nothing for as far as you could hope to see. An empty quarter, desolate and complete. Something caught his eye and he squinted to see; there was a speck almost right in the middle of the empty quarter, the words under it

25

saying: 'El Atrun'. The oasis was the start of the old road to the north once used by camel traders on their way into Egypt. There must still be people living out there, still crossing the tracks laid down by generations before them.

FOUR

The afternoon sun struck like a hammer on the sand, throwing up a layer of pure heat that hung in the motionless air. The camels were tired, more tired than he had ever seen them. A white froth dried around the edges of their nostrils and mouth. They were noisy as well, as though they thought he was ignoring their plight and were trying to get his attention. He understood their pain, but he could not make them realise that he understood. He too was tired and he too was thirsty, and so were his family, his friends and their families also.

The family was divided into different camps: those who believed that this was not right and they should return immediately into the arms of civilization, and those, like he himself, who didn't believe that this was so unusual. He had seen other years like this when the wells had run dry and the rains had been late, and so had the other older members of his family. They had all seen years like this, and they'd seen or heard of worse. He loved his animals; they were his life. He saw them growing weaker and knew that sooner or later, if things continued the way they were, the herd would have to be destroyed, or most of it, keeping just the strong ones.

The idea of moving into the villages was not a new one, but the villages had no water. They were too far away from the big towns to get water, and even if the travellers could get there, their money would be no good. They had heard the stories from others like themselves, Kabbabish, some of them. The western towns of the traders and the farmers were full to the point where special areas were being designated to these travellers, these new arrivals. He had no wish to become a part of that system. This was his home, out here with his family and his animals, his goats and his camels. Together they would face this crisis and they would reach a conclusion together, as was fitting and natural. He was not the first man to find himself subject to the will of nature, for after all, surely nature had a right to her own decisions just as everyone else had? The

27

rains would come somewhere else, for it couldn't rain everywhere at the same time; that would not be possible. Just as some years it rained heavily in one area and the ground would remain as dry as a bone less than half a day's walk away. That was nature's choice, and that was the way it had always been. That was why God had made him a traveller, so that he could move with nature. That was God's intention, to allow him to take up the best use of these rains, of the rains' will to move from one year to the next. For centuries the life of his people had been based on this, and in those years there had of course been testing times when the rains had been thin and the grass sparse and hard to find. But they had walked, and they had dug down and eventually the water had come to light and each time they had endured the test set before them.

But there was a new element that had been introduced. He himself had felt the influence of the 'Sudan' only in his more recent years. He was able to remember back to the time before they had come in their cars, with their books, giving the wells numbers and trying to decide what was best for the people. Wherever they came from, apparently in that place they knew all these things. He had laughed, as had the other old ones from the family. But the young men had seen that this future was theirs and some of them disappeared, running into the arms of the townspeople. They travelled far away to neighbouring lands, lured by riches and wealth, which no man could take with him. Did the same sun shine on this other land? Did the same stars look down from the night sky on those sons who had left their home country? Surely not, but he had seen their stars in the sky here above his land, the old land. Their stars were of different colours, and sometimes those coloured stars would flash as if in some way to impart a message across the night air. But how was it done? They moved so swiftly, too – they could cover the distance of the sky from one end to the other in only a fraction of the time between sunset and sunrise. He had spoken to other elders about these stars but they had laughed and told him that it was true they did carry the people from the other land, but that they weren't sending messages, they weren't calling to a distant god. They believed in the same God that all men believed in. This he found hard to accept. Surely if they could control the stars, then they had a different understanding of God than he had, and that most men had?

The afternoon sun had reached its zenith and was now starting to show that its mercy would return, slowly beginning to fall towards the horizon. As he walked through the small camp, with its sound of flapping tent and the *smell of tea cooking on the small charcoal stove, he could hear the camels whispering coarsely to each other, while two little boys raced in circles chasing some boyhood dispute. He loved this place. They would stay here, and either they would survive or they would perish, but God would decide that.*

FIVE

Tanner left the office and wandered round to the road that ran behind it. The narrow street had a ditch about four or five feet wide which only came in to use for a few weeks of the year when it rained. The rest of the time it was a dry trench. Three little beggar children dressed in rags crouched down together against the shade of a wall, laughing, counting out their coins. The ditch stank of stale urine and the corpse of a dead dog that lay bloated and rotting in the sun, ants crawling through its sightless eyes. On the far side of the street there was a cafeteria, part of a row of shacks. On the wooden sign that hung over the front counter, hand-painted whirls and slashes in flowing Arabic, red on green, depicted the name that was repeated in smaller letters in English underneath: El Nilain (The Two Niles). The flimsy-looking shack was held together with bent rusty nails that protruded here and there through the boards. The blue walls were worn by the sun and the dust, and looked in bad need of a new coat of paint. The café was named in homage to the union of the White and the Blue, which arrived so urgently and left so wearily as one great muddy stream sliding through this huge makeshift desert camp that had sprung from its banks. Caressing the cracked and dried mud as it went on its way, it now journeyed north, to the shores of the Mediterranean Sea: a single vein of life that cut deep through the marble heart of this malevolent and seductive land.

The sign was marked out in neon by a string of coloured striplights, mainly pink and green. From the inside of the hut a portable radio blared out drum-beating rhythms and wailing voices. Out in the street there were a few chairs and tables spread about on the freshly dampened sand, rocking unevenly. No one was using the tables. All the customers, taking their mid-morning

30

breakfast, were standing in the shadow of a structure that had been put up between the trees and the shack, trying to balance small glasses of sweet tea and the sandwiches that the man deftly sliced behind the counter. The air was filled with the sound of voices talking and calling out for food and more tea, while the young boy who carried the huge teapot scurried round filling glasses and handing out change from the pocket of his grubby smock.

The café was filled with employees from the numerous companies that were scattered round the adjoining streets. They met up here every day: drivers and messengers, clerks and general hands. The whole street was dotted with a number of cafés of a similar style to the Nilain. Tanner recognised two of the faces in the crowd. The smaller of the men waved Tanner over with one hand, while catching the tea-boy by the arm with the other. Hamdi was from the far north of the country, an amiable man with deep brown skin perhaps a shade darker than Tanner's. Thick curly hair sat in a messy bundle on his forehead. The cheerful round face was lined and showed him to be a few years older than Tanner, probably in his thirties. Tanner was twenty-six. The two had become friends while they were in the Red Sea Hills together.

Hamdi clapped him on the back and asked him where he'd been. Embarrassed by the question, Tanner said that he'd been on holiday.

'Holiday?' asked Hamdi.

'Just a short holiday. It was a long trip.'

Hamdi nodded understandingly. It had been a long trip for them all after the accident. The glass of tea arrived and was duly paid for by Hamdi, who insisted that Tanner was his guest. The other man was a southerner, tall and dark, carrying the marks that distinguished him as a member of the Dinka tribe. Mikele worked as a clerk in the accounts section of the company. He'd gained the job by making substantial use of the education offered him in the missionary schools he had attended in the South. The Catholic missionaries had been prevented from opening schools in the predominantly Muslim northern half of the country. In the pagan South they were given free reign. The influence of these missionar-

31

ies dated back to the middle of the last century and, while the advantages of this schooling system seemed to be unmatched, it later became obvious that they were in fact introducing two new barriers between the North and South: language and religion. Mikele spoke English fluently and if pressed would admit to being a Catholic.

The three men sat on rickety chairs and watched the quiet street go by. A pedlar on a donkey came past selling sugar-cane. The long sticks of cane were tied to the sides in bundles, their tips brushing the ground as the overloaded donkey stumbled along. The pedlar sat cross-legged in the makeshift saddle chewing on cane, spitting out the pulp which dotted a trail behind him. They sat and talked about general things. Mikele and Hamdi began to discuss politics in Arabic, which became too detailed for Tanner to follow. He gazed out at the street and wondered about Nina.

The cafeteria began to empty as everyone drifted back to their jobs. The owner, a small man with a large handlebar moustache, stood by the counter and surveyed his palace. The boy set down his kettle and started to rake the dust. Over his shoulder the man with the moustache spoke to Hamdi, whom he knew. Hamdi asked if he didn't recognise Tanner. The proprietor laughed, realising that he had indeed forgotten him. He walked over and slapped Tanner across the shoulders. Of course he remembered, and when was Tanner going to go to London so that he could buy him the shirts he'd promised?

'Why are you still living in this beastly country?' he added. 'No petrol, no sugar, no food, nothing, and you can leave but you stay. Why?'

'Because he likes it here,' answered Hamdi for him.

'Why should I leave?' asked Tanner.

'It would be easier for you to live abroad,' said Mikele.

Tanner looked at him sharply, thinking he had detected a trace of menace in his voice.

'Why do you say that?' he asked.

The proprietor brushed his moustache and said, 'He likes the women here better.'

He laughed loudly at his own joke and then turned to curse the boy who had stopped raking the earth. As a parting token of his opinion, the owner added, 'If you had lived here for as long as I have, you wouldn't have to ask me twice to leave.' He got to his feet and went back to his washing-up.

Mikele was a sombre man, rarely smiling easily. There was a rumour that he had once been active politically and indeed that he had played a part in the rebel army that was based in the South, fighting for autonomy. The war had come to an end and the army disbanded with the arrival of the present regime nearly fifteen years ago, but violence was erupting again. He leaned forward now to interject with urgency, 'Things are getting worse everywhere you look.'

Hamdi was struggling now for the words, his English not on the same level as Mikele's. 'There is much trouble because of these stupid secret police.' He held his hand up as though his finger were the barrel of a gun. 'Young boys are going with guns in their hands.' He shook his head regretfully.

Tanner turned his head away from this new twist in the conversation. Glancing back at the road, he saw the beggar children had started to move off. They chased each other down the street. The oldest one, a boy of about eleven, threw a rock which bounced across the road and struck the outside of a cafeteria further down. The owner came running out of his shop doorway cursing and waving a stick. The whole street stopped to watch his antics as he attempted to apprehend the villains.

It was not the first time Tanner had heard Mikele talk of war. Mikele was a supporter of Joseph Meru, the leader of probably the largest faction of rebel opposition in the South. The army had grown out of the years of increasing unrest and dissatisfaction with the power structure on the part of many southerners. The conflict was rooted in the racial and religious differences between the North and the South: the years of slavery when the black men of the South were taken by Arab traders to be sold in the Middle East. The government was run by northerners, 'red-skinned' men of Arab descent. For Mikele, Joseph Meru was a ray of hope. In a landscape of indecision and misplaced trust it seemed that there was finally someone with a clear vision and sufficient strength to deliver all that was promised. His army was going from strength to strength, and rumour had it that the government forces could do little but clear up after him on his home ground. His army controlled wide sections of the far South. Despite confusion as to which side of the political rainbow was backing him, support seemed to be growing. Listening to Mikele now, it seemed to Tanner that perhaps things were coming to a head. Like a distant roll of thunder that gathered as it approached, things were building up.

Africa had become a modern-day arena in which the superpowers could safely challenge each other for superiority. The prize on offer was the untapped wealth that lay beneath these fields of destruction.

They returned to the office and to their respective jobs. Tanner unpacked the small tin trunk that he had had with him in the Red Sea Hills. It contained all his notebooks and account ledgers and hadn't been touched since they had got back, just left on the floor behind his desk. The grubby ledgers with their curled-up corners looked dusty and strange in the confines of the air-conditioned office; they represented another place that was alien to this one. The little stub of pencil that he'd treasured so carefully for weeks he now dropped into a stationary tray along with all the others. There were a number of rock samples, some of which he hadn't bothered to pack properly and were now crumbled by the journey. Others were still intact – bits of marble that could be polished up and a piece of volcanic rock whose name he couldn't remember. In one corner of the trunk was a small cardboard box which he lifted out and carefully placed on the desk. As he lifted the lid, a large black and orange beetle crawled over the lip and fell on to the desk top. Suliman raised an eyebrow as the beetle crossed the divide and started towards him. Inside the box was a piece of coral from the Red Sea, which Tanner had bought from a tourist shop in Suakin as a present for Hammoudi. He closed the box and placed

34

it in the drawer. Suliman was trying to lift the beetle off his desk on to a sheet of paper. The insect toppled over the side, drawing a screech of surprise from Suliman who returned to his seat muttering under his breath and feeling foolish.

Tanner stayed for nearly an hour, by which time he was faced with having to start compiling his notes or else writing his report on the accident. He decided that he had done enough for the day, and left.

Outside the cafés were deserted, except for a few of the owners who sat and spat tobacco into the dirt and listened to the radio. The young boy was hosing down the forecourt. In a couple of hours everyone would be packing up for the day. It was too hot to work after about two, but by then everyone would be asleep. You couldn't argue with the dry heat, though no one seemed to want to try anyway. A hundred and ten in the shade.

Tanner's car was too hot to touch, the metal burning in the sun. Inside it was like a furnace so he wound down all the windows to let the air in. Alerted by the sound of the engine, a group of small boys crowded round Tanner's window, holding their hands out for money. Reaching into his pockets for change, he wondered where they had come from and how they had got here. So many people moved into the towns away from the poverty and the wars and the failing rains. They got here with nothing, and that was just the start. He held the handful of coppers out of the window and the crowd surged forwards. An older boy pushed his way to the front and through the gap that formed. Tanner saw another boy, probably in his twenties, coming forward. He had no legs, and moved by using his arms as crutches, rocking forward on his knuckles. He would be too late to get anything; the coins were split in the rush. Tanner took advantage of the chaos and reversed out of the parking space.

The old Fiat sped through the dusty streets and round past the palace with its high white walls and weary-looking sentries who out of boredom fiddled with the automatic weapons they held. He turned off the palace street past an old church and on to the back across the railway lines and home.

For the next week Tanner went back to the office every day. The report was duly begun and the accounts were starting to fall into shape. By the middle of the week the office was still fairly quiet. Apart from himself there was Hamdi and Suliman and the typing girl who never said anything, but whose shrill laughter now came from the far side of the room where Hamdi was busy relating a long amusing story to her. Suliman picked his nose in disapproval. Hamdi never seemed to do any work and yet he always seemed to have things done on time, which is why Suliman hated him so much. He had to work twice as hard, it seemed, and he never got anything done. Hamdi was already married, with two small daughters, so why was he the one that made the girl laugh while Suliman lived with his mother and saw no hopes of marriage in the near future at all? He wasn't getting any younger either – thirty-five next January.

Tanner looked away. He himself had been given his job as a favour; he knew there was no other reason for employing him. He was no more qualified than the typist for the job he did, but he was willing to go out in the field any time – he had no family to hold him back. He did have some mechanical ability and of course he could write reports in correct English.

He stood up to leave and Suliman put his head back down in the charts he was checking. Hamdi shouted goodbye across the room while the girl whispered something and they both giggled.

Tanner took the road that led to the river. The streets were quiet here. People came down to the cool, dark, tree-lined avenue to sleep in the breeze that came off the river. The trees were high and old, forming a canopy of leaves and branches that swayed peacefully in the wind. Taxis parked off the road with the driver's leg sticking out of the back-door window, with the doors open sometimes to let the air in. The road took him down past the yacht club, an old British frigate which had been abandoned years ago, the guns still pointing out across the river; past the university where students slept on the grass behind the big buildings of academic devotion. It could have been a different country sheltered here from the sun.

Green fields ran down from the road to the water's edge.

Farmers in baggy white cotton pants picked their way through the rows of watermelon, glancing up as the car sped past along the road with a fishtail of dust trailing behind. The road came to an end just here; the tarmac gave up and the potholes got serious. Just ahead the concrete of the new bridge jutted out from a wasteland of cactus and green puffball plants. In the shade under the bridge two obviously illicit lovers sat together and watched the river. They sat stiffly, glancing furtively about, waiting for an old man leading a donkey to pass by.

The track curved sharply away from the river just before the bridge and passed through an open gateway in a redbrick wall. Huge palm trees that must have been more than thirty years old lined the wall's interior and were dotted around the quiet lawns, their thick trunks tiered with rough scales. Their long sharp leaves rustled in the warm breeze, making a noise like the waves on a beach. In the tops of the trees weaver birds had built nests between the boughs using the thick dry foliage as support. The birds would pause at the small round entrance to their homes as they flew in and out. The drive was paved with loose pebbles which scrabbled noisily together under the weight of the car. The pebbles twisted in a double bend that came back on itself through the grass and trees of the lawns.

At the far end was a courtyard bounded on three sides by separate blocks, all built of the same red bricks as the front wall by the gate. This was part of a hostel, now used for university students in general and postgraduate and foreign students in particular.

Tanner parked the Fiat against the wall of the front building. Because of the trees, the whole area seemed cool and dark. He took the outside stairs on the nearside building and walked up easily to the third floor, the stairwell echoing with his footsteps. There was no sign of anybody about. From one of the rooms above strains of country and western music leaked past him. From the garden behind him the sound of the birds busily calling to each other followed him up the stairs.

He rang and waited for the sound of feet coming to the door. The door opened and she was standing there. Neither of them seemed sure what to do, so she stood to one side and let him in. He walked down the familiar hallway to the far room. The room was close and sultry despite the fan that spun slowly under the cracked ceiling. Nina followed him in. Pretty in a determined sort of way, she had shiny dark hair and fierce brown eyes that now looked bright even in the dimness of the room. She pushed her hair back behind her ear, repeating this action continuously with a deft twist of her left hand to lock the insistent strand in place.

'I didn't know if you'd be here,' he said. 'You said the end of the month so I thought I'd just see.' He fiddled with his car keys nervously. She pushed her hair back.

'I thought you might come by.' She spoke with soft lilting Spanish tones.

The floor was covered in clothes and books.

'When did you get back?' He waved a hand at the unpacked bag.

'Last night,' she smiled, like she used to do.

He stepped forward to meet her and she put her arms round him. He kissed her gently. 'How long have you been away, then?' he asked without taking his arms away. She shook her head and smiled again. It's nearly three months since we saw each other.'

She kissed him back. He fell into her arms. They made love on the pile of clothes that lay strewn across the floor.

When he woke up the open window was growing dark as the trees outside filled with evening shadows. He heard the screeching crescendo of the birds as they returned to their nests for the night. He went to the window and looked out, the vanishing light alive with the tiny darting forms of their nervous silhouettes. He closed the metal shutters and moved carefully back across the dark room to the door.

They had met three years ago, on the aeroplane that was bringing them both here for the first time. She was older than Tanner by about four years. She'd spent most of her childhood in South America, then she left to train as a nurse, a course she never completed. By the time they met, Nina had been working for almost ten years in one part of the world or another as a volunteer with aid agencies. She was on her way to the Sudan to join Oxfam's team. For the first few months she was stationed in Khartoum, working at the office there. It was during this time that the affair began. To say they were in love would be a simplification. True love is not a stable situation; it changes. Tanner thought back to the early days when they were living together in this flat. They were as close to love as he had ever thought possible. Love exists in a state of oblivion; when the world and its weather intrudes then it must change or fade away. They began to see less of each other as Tanner found himself spending more weeks away on excursions, and Nina was posted for a short time to the western region. When they met again they both realised that it had not survived; they were if anything only good friends.

Tanner moved into the kitchen and began to make coffee. In the cupboard behind the cups he found an envelope with photographs in it. He sat down with his coffee and flicked through them. They had been taken about a year and a half ago when he and Nina had gone for a day-trip in a borrowed motor boat. The idea was to go upstream to a quiet spot for a picnic, but the boat had become snagged in fishing lines and they eventually had to be towed back. He could remember how they had laughed. The stink of the dead fish was overpowering and they couldn't face the food they had brought with them, but they sat and laughed for nearly four hours until help came. She looked much younger in the pictures; she smiled more easily then. An intense weariness came over him as he realised that what they had then had failed to save either of them.

There was a movement behind him and she was there in the doorway, wrapped in the sheet from the bed. She looked over his shoulder. 'I'd thought I'd lost them,' she said. Tanner poured her coffee and she sat down opposite him.

'I just found them when I was making the coffee. Do you remember it?'

'Sure I do.' She took his hand and they sat and smiled at the memory.

She pulled the sheet tighter around her shoulders. Her hands were constantly moving: now she lit a cigarette, now she pushed her hair back.

'I am going back soon, you know.'

'Back to the west?' asked Tanner.

She shook her head and sipped her coffee.

'No, back to Venezuela. I am going home.' She waited for a response, then she stubbed out her cigarette.

'Where have you been these past weeks? I rang your office and they said you'd been back for more than three weeks.'

Tanner shook his head. 'I've been at home.'

'For a month? What have you been doing?' she asked, angry now. 'I thought we were friends, but you don't call me.'

Tanner shrugged in reply. He wanted to tell her that the one person he had wanted to see was her and no one else but her. At the same time she was the last person he could see; he could no longer allow himself to depend on her.

'Oh, forget it.' She waved a hand to dismiss the subject, asking, 'Are you hungry?'

They cooked a meal and ate together, talking slowly about what had been happening in the weeks since they'd last met. Nina described what she'd seen in the west.

'There's a bad shortage of food, the rains are late and if they fail again then the people are going to suffer. There's no provision for these things.' She put down her fork. 'Did you know that the reserves have been sold off? They've been exporting grain for hard currency. There are people making a lot of money out of this – it'll lead to genocide and the government does nothing. Rich land-owners have got grain but they won't sell at a loss and the government can't compete with the prices they're charging.'

Her anger turned to sorrow. 'They're all dying and no one can save them.'

The tears choked her voice. Tanner touched her hand.

SIX

Thompson's room smelled of stale air and pipe tobacco. The neon striplight cast a harsh glare across the table, behind which he hunched over figures and diagrams. The telephone was ringing, but by the time his hand came across to lift the receiver it had stopped. Tanner sat silently, staring at the wall behind Thompson's head. The wall map had gone, leaving a pale outline in the varnished wood.

Thompson put down the magnifying glass he'd been holding and reached for the pipe which sat in the large ashtray.

'So what exactly did you have in mind?'

'Well, anything really. There must be something going out.'

Thompson shook his head and pursed his lips round the pipe, while the match caught and he sucked through yellow teeth. The air filled with the sweet odour of Erinmore. The match burned his fingers and he threw it quickly into the ashtray.

'All I want is to be on a field trip, I don't mind where.' Tanner did not expect it to be easy to get himself on another expedition but there was no reason he could see to stay here.

'It's not as simple as that because we . . .' Thompson paused to attend to the flagging pipe. 'We are having to cut down all our field work, simply because of the political situation. I can't ask people to risk their lives in this job.' He pulled the pipe from his teeth and prodded the air with the stem. 'I might add the situation is not helped by what happened the last time you went out.'

Thompson was wearing a green cotton safari suit which made him look like a gamekeeper on holiday. The suit was freshly pressed with starched creases. He paused again.

'There is one thing, though. There's an American seismic expert being sent out by our people over there. I think they're worried

41

about how safe an investment they've got here. He'll be going down to Rokokoi in a few days, but I don't want to send him out alone. Maybe I could send you down with him, just to make sure he's all right.' He finished with his eyebrows raised as though expecting some kind of protest on Tanner's part.

'Just take him down and show him round?' asked Tanner.

Thompson nodded. 'That's all, just a sort of personal chauffeur. Take it or leave it – it's all I've got for the moment.'

'I'll take it. How long do you think he'll be down there?'

'A week at the most.'

It would have to do. There might be a chance once he was down there to stay on and find some more work.

Thompson had given up on the pipe and had started to dismantle it. Burnt tobacco spilled out across the desk and the papers there, and he brushed it off impatiently.

'He won't be here until next Monday so see Hamdi. He has some work for you until then, and I'll give you the details nearer the time.'

Tanner stood up and went to the door. Pulling the door to behind him on the tiny tomb-like room, he heard Thompson start to cough. The room had a feeling of death about it, cold and artificially light as though held in suspended animation.

In the other room Suliman and Hamdi were having an argument, though Suliman wasn't saying much. Hamdi was walking around throwing bits of paper from one pile to another. Apparently the girl was away to visit a sick relative. The argument had something to do with her, but with Tanner in the room Suliman was refusing to say anything. Hamdi stormed out of the room and Suliman went back to his figures.

The café was empty except for Mikele, who sat reading a newspaper. He looked up as Tanner joined him.

'You are becoming almost a regular sight again,' he smiled.

Tanner made some light-hearted reply. He mentioned the American and the job coming up. It was only after he had spoken that Tanner asked himself if he should have told Mikele. He

42

dismissed the thought; they were both working for the same company and Mikele could have found out from anyone.

Mikele held out the paper which Tanner could not read, and pointed to an article. 'They are killing each other because of the government.' The article described the shooting down of an airforce plane that was landing at Juba's commercial airport. Juba was the capital of the southern region and the airport was a prime target for the rebel armies. It sounded like they had struck quite a blow – a hundred men died, most of them replacement soldiers, government troops.

'I hear rumours everywhere I go. I see the flickering spark of the flame that will eventually engulf this whole huge country. There will be no escape for anyone, not even you, Tanner. Your solitary disdain and your detachment will not save you. You are a part of this, everyone is. It is too late for the government to ask its people to condemn this violence. The people are this violence. They are going to starve, Tanner. The government won't admit it but the people will starve and you can live here in your little new-found "home" but you won't hear anything of the dead and the slowly, painfully starving children. They are a million miles from this street where we sit and sip sweet tea. No more – when he comes everyone will wake up.'

'You think that one man can change all this?' asked Tanner.

'He isn't one man, he is a beacon, a candle around which the whole land will gather like moths.'

Tanner listened to the passion in the other man's voice and he couldn't understand how it could be so simple, so simple to believe that something like this could transform a whole country. How could anyone believe that one man could save the world?

The following morning Tanner was woken by the unexpected sound of the telephone ringing. It seemed to have repaired itself. The caller was one of the young geologists from the survey team, Zaki, a headstrong cocky lad a few years younger than Tanner. Zaki came from the sizeable Coptic community in the capital. His father was an engineer who owned his own company and had acquired a substantial degree of wealth from the machine parts which he imported and sold at extortionate prices to a starved market.

'What are you doing today?' asked the voice. Zaki was young and eager to prove it. Tanner felt tired and uncooperative.

'How did you get my number?' he asked, avoiding the question.

'I got it at the office – why? Is it supposed to be secret?' The voice seemed to falter as though suddenly unsure.

Tanner tried to change his tone. 'No, no, I was just curious, that's all.'

'So what's happening today?'

'I have to go into the office. I have some things to finish off,' muttered Tanner, trying to work out some way of avoiding this situation.

The phone erupted into laughter.

'It's Friday – the office is closed, remember? Where have you been?'

Tanner was still half asleep; but he knew he couldn't avoid the question.

'What did you want to do, anyway?'

'I have a bottle of scotch, see, so why don't I come round and pick you up?'

Tanner tried to protest.

'I'll be there in half an hour.' The phone clicked dead at the other end. Tanner had barely enough time to shower and dress before he heard the car horn sounding out in the street. Stepping off the veranda into the sun, he had to close his eyes to the brightness. The gate was hot to the touch, and he noticed how the garden had dried into a bare patch of brown stubble. He needed to take more care of it. The car was waiting just outside the gate, a Toyota with lots of shiny bits on it that glittered in the sunlight. The door opened for him and inside it was like an oven. The stereo was playing an old Beatles record. Zaki, wearing wide plastic sunglasses, put his foot down as Tanner's door closed. Through the back Tanner caught sight of a bunch of ragged youths across the street under the shade of a big tree, watching as the red car screeched away across the ruts. They howled and laughed, waving obscenely. Zaki turned up the stereo for 'Lucy in the Sky with Diamonds'.

'Where are we going?' asked Tanner half-heartedly, as the car swerved to miss a dog lying in the road. The mongrel slunk away with its tail between its legs, returning to its place when it was sure the disturbance had passed.

'We go over to Nadine's place.'

Zaki went on to explain that Nadine was some distant relative of his, who was on vacation from her college studies in the States.

'She said she wanted to meet me?' asked Tanner.

'That's what I said, man.' Zaki had the habit of adding the word 'man' to every statement he made, as a kind of flourish. Tanner wondered where it had come from.

They overtook a huge lorry on the inside and ran another red light. No one seemed to notice. The traffic lights seemed oddly out of place even in the most built-up areas in the town centre, the sombre metal poles stuck straight into the dust, where any lines or road markings had long since been covered over. The traffic seemed to find its own way. Overloaded buses yawed round corners with tailgates scraping. Men, women and children jumped on and off through the doorway when they pleased, somehow making their way through the crammed doors. Yellow taxis rattled along, gears juddering and tyres flat. Men stood on the open backs of lopsided lorries, the tails of their headcloths gripped between yellow broken teeth as they hung on to the rails and enjoyed the breeze.

The river was full of muddy swirls. Here and there along the sandy banks cars and lorries were driven into the water up to their wheel hubs for a car wash. Half-naked, skin glistening with the splashing water and the sun, boys scrubbed and polished. The chrome hub caps that decorated the dull black sides of the big lorries shimmered and dazzled; stolen, begged or won, they each fitted into place between the hand-painted messages of good will, the prayers and the raucous poetry. All the trucks had names; bastard machines spawned from imported engine cabs and spare parts, put together with a skill born from intuitive desperation.

Tanner watched the metal struts of the bridge whip by. The old pontoon structure was showing signs of age. The paint which was renewed from time to time was faded. The steel girders were streaked with rust, long trails of corrosion. Tanner had no idea how old the bridge was. He knew that during the last World War the bridge was a target for the Italian bombers which flew on air raids out of Abyssinia to the south-west. The river then would have been full of RAF flying boats. The British had been stationed here. The Italians had their own reasons for waging this particular campaign – the Sudan had always been a sore point between them and the British. The bridge had survived and now it served as the major link between Khartoum and Khartoum North, the second of the three towns clustered here. The only battle fought these days was between weary commuters on their way home in the afternoons.

Zaki turned the tape over and said something, to which Tanner just nodded.

Through the arched struts the shimmer of bronze water could be seen below. Ripples and eddies of unseen undercurrents whorled through the flow, drawing patterns like the character lines on the palm of an outstretched hand. This was the Blue Nile on the last leg of its solitary journey from the Ethiopian Highlands. The river would drift on from here down the last mile or so to the rendezvous where it met and merged with its partner and confederate the White Nile, slower moving and lighter coloured. The Blue picked up more silt because of its speed, making it darker in colour. Where they met, the line of confluent was clearly drawn in the water. The sacrifice of individuality gave rise to the birth of new strength. It was only with this combined effort that the journey across the open tracts of land to the North was possible.

Still talking, this time about politics, Zaki flipped the tape and spun the wheel, taking the car screeching round a dust plate circled by concrete blocks that passed for a roundabout.

They passed the high walls of Koba Prison. The red metal girders of the gallows were just visible, protruding like a badly hidden dark secret from behind a mask of sobriety. In the cool shadows of the brown walls children played, chasing each other in the dirt.

The room they were in was cool and dark. The window shutters were a bright green colour, the walls were white. Nadine was a slim girl of about twenty-two. Her hair was long and wavy, as though it had once been tight curls that were straightened. She greeted them both with a loud squeal, dropping a copy of *Cosmopolitan* and removing her large-rimmed spectacles in the same swift movement. She spoke with a broken American accent, with the occasional word in Arabic thrown in out of habit. Zaki undid the small holdall he carried and produced a bottle of White Horse. Nadine let out another squeal and swept across the room to the door. Calling out to the maid who had shown them in, she asked for water and ice. Through the open door past her shoulder, Tanner could see the woman nodding and turning away. Closing the door, Nadine turned back to the room.

'So we have a party, right?'

Zaki was at the record player. 'What d'you want, then?' Tanner shook his head indecisively. The Rolling Stones came on. Zaki moved away, gyrating slowly to the music. There was nowhere to sit but on the bed so Tanner sat down, the girl next to him.

'So you're the chap this *shaitan* is always talking about?'

Zaki gave a guffaw in pretend amazement. 'I am talking about him?'

The conversation, despite its mocking tones, seemed awkward. Tanner had the idea that they were speaking English for his benefit. He reached out for the glass that Zaki handed to him.

'Where is that ice?' muttered the young socialite impatiently, tossing her hair over a shoulder with a flick of the wrist.

These were the young nouveau riche of a land that was perched on the verge of an abyss of drought and widespread famine. A country where inflation figures were spiralling upwards towards damnation with ever increasing finality. Soon there would be no way back. And yet here were its brightest hopes, intelligent to a degree and possibly talented in their own way, but more than anything they were lucky. Lucky to be where they were, when outside through the air-conditioned windows poverty crawled on its knees through the urine and the dirt. There was still hope but, with every person who turned his or her back on the truth, that hope faded just a fraction more.

The far door opened and the Abyssinian maid came in with the ice.

'Ah, at last,' said the girl Nadine. The maid wore a simple blue dress that stopped just at the knee; she didn't wear a wraparound cloth *tobe* which women wore in public out of tradition. She placed the tray carefully on the low table and left quickly.

Zaki waited until she closed the door behind her. 'You've still got that ugly one working here.' He twisted his mouth in disgust.

Nadine said, 'Don't be so cheeky, boy!' but she was laughing. 'She's not that ugly.'

'She's got a face like a constipated goat – all the Habbashi women are ugly,' Zaki concluded with a dismissive wave.

The laughter made Tanner uncomfortable. Zaki slopped another two fingers of scotch into his glass, though he had hardly made an impression on the first shot.

'Do you like water in it?'

'Sure,' said Tanner, pouring the water from the plastic jug. He took a long drink from the glass. It was still a little short of midday. He decided that he should make an effort to prod the conversation along.

'What is it that you do?'

'I'm studying to be an economist.'

'Yes,' he nodded. 'I think Zaki told me.'

'I finish this year,' she went on.

'What then?'

'Then I think I want to go on and complete a doctorate.'

'Don't mess with this chick, man,' interjected Zaki, who was absently flicking through the glossy magazine she had been reading. 'She's got brains, man.' He shook his head as though in wonder, or mockery.

'What are you saying, you . . .' She seemed to be lost for words. 'And stop looking at those girls in their brassières.' She snatched the magazine out of his hand and punched him playfully in the ribs.

'What are you talking about?' He pretended not to know. She

48

shook her head and gave him a discerning stare. 'You know what I mean.'

Tanner examined his glass. Nadine began to compose herself, giving a nervous laugh and taking a sip from her drink. She brushed her hair out of her eyes needlessly and brought her gaze round to meet Tanner's. 'I thought we were talking about you, anyway.'

'That shouldn't take long,' said Tanner in an attempt to break into the right mode. He felt annoyed at having been dropped into this set-up. It was as if he'd been brought here just for their amusement. He was weary of the game so it mattered little to him. He sipped again from the cut-glass tumbler and took a closer look at the girl to whom he had been lured. Nadine had noble blood in her, or so she claimed. Her mother was of Egyptian descent, and the Pharaohs were somewhere in the deep misty past of blood ties and extended family trees. This Egyptian link gave her a position in society and her pale complexion: she had light-brown milky skin and features that were just a touch too narrow to be purely sensual, while there was a hint of harshness in her obsidian eyes.

She began to tell him about university life. The picture she drew was a mixture of puritanical pride in her beliefs, and blatant ignorance of her surroundings and disdain for the future of the land. She took what society gave her without question, and in return she cast judgement from on high. When she spoke of her future she didn't mention the Sudan, as though there was no chance for these two concepts to meet: the concept of hope, and the concept of land. Sudan, 'Land of the Blacks', where its people inherited an environment that had to be tamed with every new life destined to walk across its face and sleep in its arms and breathe its desert winds and drink its rivers' blood. Where the dictates of slavery bound their hands with history. There were riches beyond any man's dreams, riches enough for every man, woman and child who asked, but first the heart of the beast had to be understood. The answer to this dilemma lay out beyond these cool air-conditioned palace walls. The answer lay in the dust, in the rust that ate through the railway lines, in the cancerous holes that gaped through the city streets. It lay hidden in the minds of these

49

inheritors who wandered unaware between the inheritance of history's division, and the sad empty promises of someone else's future.

There were other people arriving soon, Zaki informed them, mentioning several names, though none of them rang any bells with Tanner. They were all part of a small social group, isolated by their background. Somehow they had been exposed to another world, outside the one they lived in every day. Another world with a different set of values and traditions. A world with problems of its own. They were living in a Third World country, but their hopes and dreams were firmly embedded in the western world, the 'first' world. They heard about the problems the people had there, about the unemployment, the racism, the inequalities and the injustices. But they were blind to them, deaf to their warning shouts. They saw wealth in the streets, on their TV screens. They yearned for the freedom and the choice. They ignored the plight of those around them. Outside the streets were filled with people who had travelled hundreds of miles from their homes and villages in search of something more. They lived in cardboard shanty towns and watched the cars drive by.

Tanner realised that he wanted to be alone. Besides, he really had nothing to say at all. He put his glass down on the table in front of him and stood up.

'I think I'll be going.'

They protested – how could he go so early? He hadn't met the others yet. Tanner said he was tired. 'Anyway I'm not very good company today.'

Zaki offered to drive him back, but Tanner had expected this and was therefore prepared to turn him down. He would get a taxi – it was no trouble.

Nadine walked across the room with him, her bare feet silent on the tiled floor. 'You will come to see us again, won't you?'

Tanner held the door with one hand. ''Course I will, I'm sure there's a lot you haven't told me about the States.'

She smiled at that. Tanner said he'd see himself to the door, which closed behind him. Tanner found himself back in the hallway which was warm after the air-conditioned bedroom. From behind the door he could hear the strains of the record player still blaring away. The hallway was suddenly quiet in reply. At the far end of the long marble-tiled floor the girl Maria sat in a small upright wooden chair. In her hands she held an embroidery frame, pushing the needle back and forth through the cloth: yellow flowers with green leaves. She didn't look up as Tanner went by. He hurried along the corridors and out into the sepia landscape that shrivelled like celluloid in the midday sun.

The spin of the fan blades seemed wildly exaggerated. Papers flapped nervously across the heaps of accumulated documents strewn over the big desk. The man behind the desk was not the same one as last time, though it was the same office. The view was the same: the open window and the shaded veranda that faced north, the dusty fronds of cobwebbed palm trees that nodded narcotically in the courtyard below. The last man had been a little overweight – sweating, Tanner remembered, despite the furious ceiling fan. The fact was that his appearance had been misleadingly disarming. The outward jollity concealed a perfect blankness where bureaucracy reigned: the misconception of disorder whereby procedure implies authority and efficiency, neither of which exist within such parameters.

The new man was different. There was no mistaking his appearance for his character. His crooked smile seemed to match the knuckles with which he now rolled his cigarette. The lopsided spectacles distorted the jaundiced eyes. The thin plume of smoke that rose from his fingers was sliced apart by the fan blades and sent scurrying to the four corners of the room.

Tanner felt insecure in this room where the door behind him was wide open to match the window. The man smiled until a *murrasalla* appeared with a tin tray on which there were two glasses of sweet mint tea. He placed the glasses on the table and the man behind the desk threw a coin on to the plate.

'So.' He pushed his glasses further back on his nose and shuffled through his papers. 'You have asked for this interview in order

51

that you might put your case for citizenship in person. Is that correct?' He looked up.

'Yes, that's it,' said Tanner with a quick nod.

'Aha.' He rolled the sound as though savouring it, drawing it out like a delicate thread, conscientious as an arachnid perfectionist.

'The problem of course has not changed, as I believe you must be aware.' The eyes flickered up. 'Your situation has not changed, I presume?'

'No.' The question was superfluous; the details were all on paper, but it was a necessary part of the preliminary fencing.

The conversation was taking place in English at Tanner's request, as he lacked confidence in his Arabic. He would rather not have had to ask for such a favour but his command of the language stretched only as far as fairly light conversation and he wanted to be clear about the details here. It was a point against him, he felt, and added to his unease.

'Tariq El Mirghani.' The official read from the form. He slid some more papers aside. 'But your British passport is in another name.'

'It's there on the birth certificate. I was given two names.'

'Yes, of course.' He paused, sipped noisily at his tea and placed the glass carefully back on the blotter, which was spattered with various marks. 'The problem, as I'm sure you realise, is that we cannot issue a citizenship for you if you retain your British nationality. We cannot permit you to be a part-time citizen.' He tried to smile at his own humour but the result was less than convincing and resembled an expression of pain more than anything else.

'I would have to surrender my passport to you.'

'It is a long procedure and the outcome is by no means certain. You would be unable to travel out of this country for another five years and of course you may be called upon to perform National Service.'

'You mean join the army?' Tanner could feel where all this was leading. He now recognised the difference between this man and the one he had spoken to last time. That man had been an idiot, a victim of a system that he could not comprehend, helpless and

52

useful for only the most menial of tasks. A plodding workhorse. This man on the other hand was as lithe as a rat, sliding through the stygian channels with ease. He made the best use of the system; he was not a victim but a predator, encouraging the confusion within which he worked.

'The political situation in the South, as I'm sure you know, is unstable at the moment and it is quite likely that you would be called upon.'

Tanner waited.

'There are of course simpler methods of reaching the same outcome. In your case, I mean, the law seems to be rather an annoying inconvenience, nothing more than an oversight on the part of those high and mighty judges.'

'How much of an inconvenience are we talking about?' asked Tanner pointedly.

The man shrugged comfortably. 'At this stage perhaps it is better that you go away and give the matter some thought.' He reached for a pencil. 'I'm sure we can reach an agreement when you are decided.' He handed over a scrap of paper. 'This is my number. Ring me and we can talk about the matter in more detail.'

Tanner found himself surprised by the ease with which the offer was made. The meeting was concluded and he stood up to leave.

'It is quite funny to think that anyone who had the options open to you would have left this country a long time ago, and yet here you are knocking at the door to be let in.' The comment was made with what seemed to be genuine curiosity.

'Perhaps we are all so busy trying to get what we haven't got that we don't realise the true value of what we're holding in our hands?'

Tanner left the office and walked round along the open veranda, fresh warm air sweeping gently along. It was almost two o'clock and people were starting out for home, the day's work over. The route to the stairs took him past the open window of the room he had just left. He glanced in and was surprised to find the room completely empty. The sound of laughter drifted up from the grassy lawns that decorated the courtyard below. Someone was sleeping beneath a tree. People were dotted about talking.

The steps led down to the familiar sand in the drive. Tanner went to the high metal gates that were stuck open. The old gateman returned his nod. He never got out of his seat, an old metal seat with bits of rope hanging off telling of innumerable repairs. By his side a smooth brown staff and a lame brown mongrel were his defences. He ejected a long stream of reddish-brown spittle through a gap between his front teeth. With his tongue he adjusted the lump of tobacco that he held in the pouch behind his lower lip and wiped his grey whiskers dry.

Tanner spent the rest of the day wandering through the markets in town. He bought a few vegetables, some fruit. It was hot and humid. From on top of their mounds of grapefruit and watermelon the vendors sprayed water over the fruit to keep them looking fresh. They called out, trying to attract trade, even calling to customers at neighbouring stalls to undercut their rivals. The place was full of noise and movement of people and animals: donkeys and goats; children scampering about between the slow-moving crowds, spilling baskets; fast legs – and even faster hands – darted here and there, eyes like hawks after easy pickings. Fellow vendors laughed at a neighbour's plight. Swearing to himself, the stricken man returned to his stall to count his losses. The flies swarmed through the carcases that hung in the meat market. The butchers in blood-stained aprons flicked at them with horsehair whips; the flies were oblivious.

Tanner left the markets behind, walking through the small back streets towards the town mosque and the bus ranks. These streets were open to the sun; no trees were planted here, for here no visiting dignitaries would be brought, no presidential motorcade would drive through these streets. People used the ditches for toilets – what else was there to use? It was too hot to walk far. The sand crept through his open sandals to collect between his toes where the sweat turned it to grime. The breeze cooled his body through the thin cotton shirt he wore, except under his arms where the sweat grew in a damp crescent moon. He stubbed his foot on a discarded brick that was part of the assortment of rubble scattered across the open space like an uneven carpet.

Against the low wall of the mosque the lepers sat in a ragged line

54

with tin bowls held in fingerless hands. They waited for passers-by to pause for a moment in their haste and drop their bronze coins into the bowls. Their eyes gazed far away, their lips mumbling prayers to the god who had condemned them to this existence, begging forgiveness and release. The sound of their recital was barely audible above the cacophony of cars and buses, the rattling gears and the ringing bicycle bells. They rocked back and forth against the wall, as though willing themselves into another world, away from this one which had judged them so cruelly. The wall reeked of stale urine and shit. Tanner threw a handful of change into the nearest bowl and moved quickly past.

From the back of the Toyota pick-up bus, Tanner could look out and see the same lepers still rocking in their trance. A small boy, who couldn't have been more than twelve, jumped on the tailgate, as the 'box' lumbered away through the deep ruts in the dust. Between his teeth hung a cigarette and over his shoulder was slung a small plastic bag. He was the conductor. Hanging on to the aluminium bar with one hand, he waved to the other boys as they shouted and cursed, laughing to each other. In another world they would be at school eating school dinners, worrying about home-work and their future careers. Here they had it all: riding the tailgates during the day, gambling away the nights, getting high sniffing petrol. Swinging his legs over the gate, the conductor sat down and rattled the change in his bag and without saying a word the passengers reached for their money. The boy rode the bumps and ruts as he counted the coins, never needing his hands to steady himself. The passengers bounced up and down on the bare wooden benches. The sun peeked through tears in the green canvas that covered the back of the pick-up. In their wake the canvas fluttered against the metal frame and dust trailed them in a billowing swirling cloud.

Tanner tugged at the string tied to the Chinese bicycle bell that told the driver when to stop. He got out and watched the Toyota take off again, the suspension so overloaded that the tail hung inches above the uneven road. He walked the last hundred yards or so to his house. The gate creaked with familiarity, while the garden looked more neglected than ever. He placed the bag of fruit and vegetables that he'd bought in the refrigerator, without removing them from the bag, and took out an old bottle that had once held Haig whisky, according to the label, but was now used to chill water. He unlocked the door to his room and went into the dim interior. Gulping at the ice-cold water, he flicked the switch that set the white-painted blades of the fan revolving. He lay back on the bed and watched the three blades become indistinguishable in the blur. He placed the bottle by his head on the floor and closed his eyes. Tanner fell asleep and dreamed of sand.

SEVEN

Lights flickered through the darkness, the soft murmur of voices creeping across the sleeping sands. A breath of breeze flapped at the heavy cloth, nagging insistently for a moment before it blew away across the lacerated plains. The desert exhaled, content perhaps in the respite that evening brought. The sun had long since sunk from the sky, dropping away from the edge of the world like a stone. Not a moment too soon, was the whisper that ran through the cracked earth and gravel. Having endured another harsh insistent burning, the stones that had blistered in the heat now cooled slowly and returned to their normal size. From within their shadows, cracks and crevices, lizards and scorpions emerged to seek out what they could under the mournful glare of the hunter's moon. Darkness hung over them like a cloak, warm and invisible. The sand began to shift, uneasy in its sleep.

An ageless place which lay exhausted in its efforts to endure the eternal desolation to which it had been condemned. The sparkling rivers that once trickled and bubbled their way through this land had long since dried up into the furrows of scars that traced their lines across this toothless parchment. All the trees and grass that had rolled across open savanna plains were gone, shrivelled and dried as the soil turned sour. The land had shed its skin and now lay bare for all to see the truth. Only the wind and the stars lived here. So many millions of years, in the blink of an eye, in the space of a heartbeat, a million lifetimes passed by only as a sigh of oblivion in dereliction.

The young boy looked down over the camp of shelters that were spread out below. He was leader of this family now, the responsibility fallen to his shoulders. His father was dead and he was the oldest male. His father had been killed by raiders, camel thieves from the Rizayqat, who rarely came this far north. Usually they stayed much further south. Hardly ever had he even heard of them straying from the outer reaches of the western hills. But they had come, and they had brought death with them. The family had been camped for the night, just over a day's march south from the oasis at El Atrun.

57

The Rizayqat had come in when the camp had settled down, creeping through the warm evening to where the camels were tethered. One of the camels jumped, which was rare as the thieves usually know their business well. They can steal silently and efficiently, generations of experience behind them. Camels could be sold for a good price, and those that roamed these lands were once among the best in the Arab world. You could buy food and drink and modern weapons with the money.

Hearing the noise, the boy's father had got up to investigate. Together with his oldest son, he gave chase to the raiders but the Rizayqat were better equipped. They carried modern Russian submachine guns and they cut down the man and his son with these Kalashnikovs. The raiders escaped into the sand.

The young boy picked himself up out of the dirt where he lay mourning his brother and his father. He collected the old rifle from where it had dropped next to his father. He tapped the barrel carefully to clear it of any sand and small stones that might have lodged themselves inside. Resting the rifle over one shoulder, he pulled the cartridge belt over the other and set off.

It took him three days and nights. He never stopped anywhere for more than an hour at a time. At night he would sit and cry, lying under the velvet stars he would struggle to keep his sobs silent. He was twelve years old.

On the evening of the third day he saw smoke again. He knew he was close up, less than a mile away. They were in no hurry, these bandits. Who was there, after all, to give chase? Just a young boy, and no camels or horses, so why worry?

The boy crawled on his belly like a snake up the hard bare rock of the boulder at the end of the wadi. He peered over the rim and he could see the flicker of flame. He felt his belly tighten. He could hear voices now, and he moved closer. There were three – no four – men. The camels were tethered to a peg in the ground, on the far side of the small fire, around which he could now see the dark outlines of the men. They sat around in the open, talking and laughing. They were passing food and drink between them, and the boy hadn't eaten for days. He moved back down the rock and lay on his back staring at the stars; they looked so peaceful.

He knew it would be impossible to do what he had come here for. He had forced himself on, day after day, never knowing if he would catch up with them, never knowing if he would get the chance to avenge the blood that had been spilled. But now that it all appeared to be within his grasp, he could see *that it was impossible. All he had was a single-shot rifle while they had Kalashnikovs. He was one, they were four. His mind was in turmoil, but his body was exhausted, and soon he was asleep.*

When he woke it was late into the night. He was cold, exposed without protection from the stars, and he shivered. He crawled back up to the rim and peered over. The camp was silent. Now was his chance, while they were all asleep. He placed four cartridges on the rock in front of him and stuck a fifth between his teeth for luck. He loaded the first shell into the breech, and aimed for the first man.

EIGHT

The fingers sliced through the pale green water, cutting an envelope through which the slim brown body slipped easily. The splash startled a large monitor lizard perched on the far side of the pool. It broke its motionless mould and scurried away. Ripples made for the side and Tanner slid through the warm water. Half-way down the length of the pool, he stopped and began to tread water. His breath was jerky and laborious. Probably too much smoking, or not enough exercise. The chlorine stung his eyes and his body felt tired and old. He started again, taking long gliding strokes.

The pool was deserted except for Tanner. He liked to swim and at one time used to make a point of getting to the pool at least three times a week. If he came round in the mornings he often had the whole place to himself. It was an open pool inside the University, overhung by huge thirty-foot trees. Sometimes as now there was a rake man who dragged the pool with a net on a long pole. He strolled along the sides stroking the surface of the water with his net. Tanner reached the far side and forced himself to turn and go back without resting.

It was two months now since he had arrived back from the desert. The American had been delayed and there was little else for him to do. He was half-way through the report he was writing. He didn't want to hand it in. The death of the student girl was still on his mind. The truck had overturned because they were in too much of a hurry. There had been nothing to do. It could have been avoided. Hector had been in overall charge of the trip but it was Tanner's job to make sure the trucks had been checked. It was Tanner who had hired both trucks and drivers.

They had been camped on a hillside overlooking the ghost town of Suakin. Once an important link in the trade routes, it now was

60

slowly falling into ruin, inhabited by wild cats and pilgrims and the soft swell of the Red Sea that blows through the phantom windows of the large abandoned houses.

The truck was overloaded and they had been driving too fast, down the rocky track to the flat plain that stretched away east. They were on their way home. The truck hit a pothole or a rock, or the axle gave way first – it wasn't clear. Tanner was ahead in the Land Rover driving fast; they were winning the race. There was a shout from one of the men in the back and he looked up at the mirror in time to see the truck cartwheeling down the hillside.

When they got to the wreck there was blood all over the place. The driver's cab was smashed up; and the driver had been flung through the open door. There were bodies all strewn across the sand. There was the slow awakening of groaning, and in the stunned aftermath only one figure didn't make a sound. She shouldn't have been in the back – she should have been in the Land Rover. She was all broken up and crushed. The truck had rolled over her, almost cutting her in two. Her half-naked body lay in the brown dust.

They had to drive for almost a day with the body in the back of the Land Rover covered with just a blanket, one of the boys keeping the flies off, before they got to a police station at Port Sudan which refused to take the body. They then had to go to the army morgue where an argument broke out between opposite factions in the group. Some of them thought it best to bury the girl where the death had occurred while others wanted the body to go back to her family. They left the body with the police. Tanner had felt guilty at the time, though what he could have done was not clear. He would straighten it all out for the report, eventually.

He saw Nina from time to time, though he never stayed long. Part of him he knew, would like to go back to the domestic life they had shared at the beginning. But he knew that he no longer could face that; the innocence of those days was somehow missing now. They spent the night together, but it wasn't the same as it had been at the beginning. Neither of them would admit it; they needed each other too much.

He would go to Caesar's place more often now – he needed the anonymity of the moon-eyed girl whose name he could never remember. Often he went there just to drink. He would pay for the whole night and they would sit there and she would listen while he talked and drank the rough spirit that brought tears to the eye. She didn't understand English, but she would sit quietly and not interrupt. Often the whole night would pass without them making love. He had no desire for her, he just needed her companionship. She would fall asleep while he talked.

Hamdi would cover for him at work, telling Thompson that Tanner was redoing some charts for him at home. Tanner immersed himself in cheap novels to pass the time. He longed to read something worth while, but trash was easier; it was like a dose of anaesthetic, the effect fading with time. It was winter now, and Tanner found that he preferred to read at night when it was colder and there was no need to keep the fan on. It was cool enough to sit outside, where he could see the stars on clear nights, which was almost always.

Gradually his day turned round and he stayed up later and later, reading in the long quiet nights when there was no interruption. No sounds from the neighbouring houses, no cars passing by. It was dark and silent. As he read by the light of a small lamp, the nights became longer. He would sleep later in the day to make up for the hours lost. Eventually he reached the point where he would spend the day sleeping in his room, dark with the shutters closed. He would wake late in the evening, when most people were making their last call on friends or eating their supper. Tanner would wake and eat a little bread and cheese, a few olives. Sitting in the courtyard at the back of the house, he would listen to the world as it prepared to end another day. The cars passing by became fewer, the noises from over the wall would reduce, until he could hear the whispers of his neighbours drift into sleep-filled silence.

His clock had been turned around completely. There was nothing he wanted from the daylight. He left the world to carry on as he knew it would; all he needed could be provided by the night. Tanner found that no matter how much sleep he got, he would still be tired. He could sleep for twelve hours at a go, regularly, but still he would feel an intense fatigue. At first he thought he'd screwed up his body clock – wasn't that what it was called? At the back of his mind a nagging doubt told him that it was more than just a form of jet-lag. He had no interests any more, he hardly spoke to anyone. Days would pass by when he would speak to no one at all. There would be no reason to leave the house. There were times when he would catch himself sitting alone staring into empty space, his attention caught by the sound of voices from the neighbouring house, a snatch of a conversation: a man talking to his wife, or the mother shouting to the children. She was an old woman, though the children were not yet into their teens. Tanner had seen them playing in the street.

They would run about trying to hit each other with a small rubber ball, while one would try to build a tower from a pile of flat stones. Inevitably the pile of stones would keel over just before the final one was put in place, or the ball would find its target and the teams would change places. When a car came by they would chase it out of their pitch, shouting and jeering at the driver. Other kids came from all over the area, the street filled with their noise as they darted around, barefoot in the dusty road. Until the light faded, when they retreated into the shadows of the sparse streetlights to smoke cigarettes and boast about their exploits. At night his neighbour's children would be subjected to their mother's wrath. Tanner would listen to her high-pitched tones and their mumbled defence in reply.

Once a week Tanner would take a taxi into town to buy food from the market, check the post office for letters and see to general things. He usually set off early. It wasn't far but he liked to get to the market before the heat of midday. Often he ended up in one or other of the small bookshops that sold books in English. He enjoyed the dark cool interiors with the hum of the air-conditioning, which made it almost too cold, and the smell of paper and ink. He could spend hours wandering up and down the aisles, glancing at the titles on display. The selection would rarely change; he knew most of the books and sometimes would even notice when a book had been moved, or that one was missing that had been there on his last visit. Tanner would shuffle along back and forth in search of something he could buy. Again and again he would sift through the shelves in case there was something he had missed. They were all similar in a way – gaudy covers with brightly painted pictures of a warplane from the forties, shiny pistols, heroes with blond hair and welded steel chins. Often he would become aware of the shop assistant's watchful gaze as he surveyed yet another lithe female figure scantily clad in some kind of ridiculous satin outfit. The cover picture never had anything to do with the story. Eventually Tanner would get bored of looking at the same books so he would settle on whatever caught his eye at that moment. Sometimes the shopkeeper would grow impatient if it was his dinnertime soon, and he would start to pull the metal shutter down at the front of the shop or jangle his keys to indicate that he wanted to go.

On one of these visits into town Tanner had just decided that he would not find anything new. He gave up all hope and left to get home before the rush hour started. It was already late. He came out of the shop and turned to walk along the covered pavement. As he turned, his eye caught a figure getting out of a car parked in front of the bookshop. It was the girl Nadine. Tanner dropped his eyes to the ground and walked on, hoping he hadn't been noticed. He had just reached the step that led off the paved area and on to the hot sand and stones when a hand touched his shoulder.

'Hello there,' she said.

Tanner smiled and said hello back to her. She was wearing a pale blue *djellabia*. Loose and shapeless, it hung down to her painted toes, her slim dainty feet in flat leather sandals.

'I thought it was you,' she said, glancing at the bag he was carrying. 'Been doing some shopping, I see.' She slipped the sunglasses off her Cleopatra nose and waved the beggar children away. 'Where are you off to now?' She stepped off the sunburned street into the shade of the pavement as Tanner explained he was going home.

'Where is your car?' she asked, and he told her the Fiat was being repaired.

'Let me give you a lift, then,' she said. 'My car's across the street

– can you wait there a minute? I just want to pick up some things and I'll be right over.'

She gave him the keys, saying, 'It's okay, I won't bite you.' She laughed and turned to walk off past the shopfronts before disappearing into a jeweller's. Tanner let himself into the car, which was a Toyota or a Datsun – some kind of Japanese car, anyway. It looked clean and new inside, and the windows were tinted green. He was just settling down when the door opened and she slipped into the driver's seat.

'It's boiling in here – why don't you put the air-conditioner on?' She flicked a switch and dusty air that soon turned cool blew into his face. A poor boy held out his hand and stared mournfully through the window at her. She ignored him as she started the engine and pulled out of the parking space.

'You know,' she said, adjusting the mirror and slipping on her sunglasses again, 'Zaki explained why you had to leave that time. He said you had an appointment.'

'That's right,' said Tanner. He hadn't told Zaki that he had any kind of appointment, but he was grateful that he had made an excuse for him – not that he cared either way.

'But that doesn't explain why we haven't seen you in all these weeks. Are you hiding from us?' Through the cool green glass the traffic was held up for a donkey which was snorting and kicking its hind legs in the noonday sun. A pedlar ran after the beast trying to calm it and save his wares. Taxi drivers leaned out their windows and waved their arms, cursing both man and beast.

'Why should I be hiding?' he asked, staring out the window, feeling her eyes on the back of his head.

'Where have you been, then? There aren't that many places for you to go.'

Tanner wondered how old she was. She seemed very curious, or perhaps she wasn't. It was hard to tell.

'I thought you'd be back at college by now,' he said.

'Next Friday,' she answered, her accent faltering. 'I can't wait to get out.'

Tanner glanced over; she was smiling.

'If it's so bad, why don't you go for good?'

65

She waved one hand in the air. 'I don't know, but I'm telling you, if I find a way to stay there after my course finishes, that's it.' She laughed as though she knew she could find a way. She turned to Tanner again. 'But what about you? Why are you here? You're lucky, you have a British passport, don't you?'

Tanner nodded.

'Then why don't you get out of this dump, and move to London? I'd be off like a shot.'

Tanner thought about why he'd come here. There seemed to be no questions in her mind about living in Britain, about the difficulties that might occur. Maybe he should tell her about the inequalities he had seen, the poverty and the racism. But she could say that all of those things existed here, and worse. So what could he tell her? That she wouldn't belong? What would that mean to her? She could buy a car like this, though she wouldn't need the tinted windows. You only saw what you wanted to see; wealth provided its own protection.

'I used to live there, but I thought I'd like to see what it was like here.'

She laughed. 'Have you not seen enough yet?'

He had probably seen a lot more than she had. He had travelled to places that were not even marked on maps. He had seen the land, and met a lot of people. People who welcomed him to their homes, gave him food to eat and tea to drink, people who wanted to know where he had come from, why he was here. Village people, town people.

'But surely you are changing the subject. I asked you if you were avoiding us.' By us, she meant herself.

No he lied, he wasn't avoiding her, why should he? She shrugged, and without taking her eyes off the road said, 'How should I know what your reasons are?'

They reached the road outside Tanner's house. He climbed out of the car on to the hot sand and, leaning in, picked up his bag.

'So long. Thanks for the ride.'

She said she might see him before she left. Tanner said yes, he might come round. She laughed out loud, pushed the car into gear and accelerated away, dust and stones kicking out from under the tyres. He could see her hand waving through the rear window before the car turned a corner out of sight.

Pinned to the door Tanner found a note from one of the company drivers. The phone wasn't working, and he was wanted at the office as soon as possible. Tanner pulled the message off the wall and went inside. He tried the phone but it was still dead. He wondered how long it had been like that. It wasn't unusual; in fact it was more common for the phones to be out of order than not. It was too late to get to the office before they shut down for the day. It was two o'clock in the afternoon.

After eating, Tanner took a shower. The cool water washed the sweat and grime off his body, out of his hair. His legs felt shaky and weak and he sat down on the floor, letting the water stream down the back of his head. The pressure of the drops of water felt soothing. Tanner sat in the shower until he began to shiver with cold. Turning off the tap, he wrapped a towel round his waist and padded across to his bedroom, leaving a trail of wet footprints across the red tiles.

He lay down on the bed, the water from his body collecting into rivulets that ran down his sides and made dark stains on the sheets. The evaporating water slowly began to turn to sweat. He could not sleep; his mind felt uneasy. All the quiet and solitude of the past few weeks had been disturbed. The girl Nadine – he could not make her out. He had shown her no interest whatsoever, but she still pursued him. What did she want? Maybe he just amused her with his disillusionment. She must, thought Tanner, be one of the most light-headed people he had ever met. But was there something he had missed, some detail that she kept hidden behind the façade. She was playing with him. So what? Maybe her interest could have its advantages.

Then there was the letter from the office. That meant there was work to be done somewhere, or maybe they had decided he was too much trouble to keep around. Would they fire him? Why not? He was not overly qualified. One A-level and an unfinished HND; there were a lot of people about with better letters after their names. He did have experience, though; he could handle work teams, he was useful in the field; the engineers liked him, he

67

worked hard. Over the years he'd picked up most of the work despite the fact that he had no formal training. It wasn't hard, you just had to concentrate. He could handle things like seismic shots, and supervise core taking: they just had to say where. Usually he followed behind the survey team with the engineers and the labourers. It was hard work, but it kept him busy.

Tanner dozed on and off, reading a little. The time passed slowly. At dusk he made some tea and sat out in the yard, the sand still warm. Darkness fell and the stars hid behind the glow from the street lights. High up against the sky, the green and red lights on an airliner moved silently. The plane began its slow descending arc towards the ground. Thc tca was cold. Tanner realised that for the first time in weeks he was bored.

NINE

From the roof you could see out across the sea of flat-topped houses. In the distance the streetlights ended and there was only darkness beyond; no lights in the sky except the pink neon lights that marked the tower of a mosque.

Was there a reason for his being there at this time? If there was any explanation for his coming here then it surely lay in the events of his past. There was a sense in which he had betrayed his own beliefs. He had come here to start a new life, to find out if he had a home here. Yet here he was isolated and alone, through his own choice. The girl's death had been his responsibility; he was in charge of overseeing that the trucks were maintained. In this particular case he had made a mistake; something had been overlooked and someone had paid the price for his oversight.

The girl's death was a turning point for him, making him realise that he couldn't go on without good reason. He had come here with reason, but somewhere along the way it had been mislaid. When he had first arrived he believed that he could make a go of it, but now he had been caught between the narrow walls of this would-be metropolis: a savage burlesque in which the war and the starvation were nothing more than sideshow stands.

Nina had been the answer in the beginning. Together they had discovered the town and the culture which were alien to both of them, but to which Tanner felt he must have some kinship. In their love he found salvation. He had been left standing still when she took off and actually did, or tried to do, something. She had the strength to sit and nurse a child back to life. He'd seen her working in a field station last Easter when by chance they were in the same region. She sat there crouched on a wooden stool, a scrawny child with bones like a chicken wrapped in her arms, coaxing it to eat.

Though he was in no sense a believer, there was something almost divine in the way she worked, moving among the wounded and the dying and the naked and the homeless like some kind of angel.

In the street below the headlights of a car moved slowly down the road, coming almost to a standstill before rolling carefully through a particularly large pothole. The car drew up outside a house, the engine still running in the unlit street. There was a pause, a light came on over the door and a figure appeared in the doorway. She shouted something to the person in the car. The car rolled slowly away and the girl went back inside.

When he was born he was given another name. The name that his father gave him but which he never retained. It was easier to hold on to his 'English' name at school and later at work, with his friends. If there is an importance in the naming of things then it is that the name should be appropriate. The only thing Tanner could say for sure was that his name wasn't Tanner. When he had first come here he had tried to revert to the old name, the one his father had left him. The process of names is habit-forming and it is not easy to change after twenty-five years. He eventually settled for dropping his first name and just using his surname. This process somehow produced the distance required. His past was bound up in that name and he felt the need to isolate his past.

Tanner had no wish to return to the little house in Leeds with the smell of dog in the worn-out furniture and the stain of compromise in the peeling wallpaper. The confines of the narrow living-room reeked of regret. The marriage had not worked out though neither of the participants was willing to admit it. They would carry on like so many thousands of couples inside the low light of lampshade glow. The dark hall would remain out of sight and life would go on. The dogs would chew the arm off the sofa again and the gas bills would be paid eventually and Christmas would come round every year to mark another, and he would go off to work every morning and she would sit in and wait for him so she could heat up the meal and serve it.

Tanner was twenty-six years old and all he knew about his life was that he didn't want to go back over any single moment of it. Not for pain or sorrow or the happiness that was there. There was

70

no time to go back, and there was no indication of any direction in which to proceed.

It was still early enough to go out. Tanner took the car and turned towards town.

There was a series of social clubs in Khartoum. Each one had its own defined section of the community to which it catered and each one had its own position in terms of prestige and status afforded to its members. The boundaries that segregated and defined these places were based on factors of religion, class and race. The indigenous Greek, Arab and Coptic communities all had their own little clubs where they could meet their own people, as did many other factions. The prestige of belonging to these family affairs was hard to define. At the top of the points scale were the expatriate clubs: the American club where people of all creeds and origins could order Sloppy Joes in their best imitation drawl. The German and Italian perhaps to a lesser degree, but possibly the most exclusive one was the Sudan Club, where the British could come and go with ease. They could sit by the pool and sip iced lemonade, slip into bikinis hidden from dirty Arab boys' eyes by high walls and trees. Until recently it was possible to discuss the whys and wherefores, the 'us' and 'them', over a glass of imported beer.

Tanner had joined the club when he had first arrived, having been introduced by some of the company people. Then Nina had taken a liking to the place, though she could go only as his guest. Finally he stopped going, preferring the quieter pool at the University for his swimming. Tonight it was perhaps only curiosity that brought him back.

Pulling up outside, Tanner was surprised at the number of cars parked against the whitewashed walls. Inside he found Henry Cale on the patio. Henry was a big round-faced man who had something to do with the British Council.

'Ah, long time no see,' he slurred, waving a hand in Tanner's direction.

What's going on tonight?' asked Tanner.

71

Henry Cale tutted in irritation. 'Some amateur dramatic thing, Noël Coward play, I think. Fancy a Scotch, my boy?' he asked, leaning forward with a sly grin. He lifted his hand from the pocket of his jacket to reveal a half bottle of whisky. He called out to the man who was supposed to be serving but was slumped at the counter staring into space. The glass of soda water arrived and Henry poured a healthy measure into Tanner's glass.

'Say when,' he said, not stopping until the glass was brim full.

Henry Cale was gay; Tanner knew this from an early encounter when he had confessed his desire. Since then they had become friends of a sort. Henry could be witty and incisive in his wry observations of life; he also seemed to have come to terms with the fact that Tanner was not interested in going to bed with him.

'Nothing worse than amateur dramatics. Excruciating to watch these people, all the would-be Oliviers and Scarlett O'Haras hanging out the left-over laundry of their lives.' He shook his head in dismay.

'How about a game of snooker?' suggested Tanner.

'Why not?' said Henry. 'Though I doubt I could even find the table, let alone the pockets, at this stage of the evening.'

The snooker room was dim and quiet. The whole club, it seemed, was watching the play. A sign on the wall advertised it for anyone who had not caught on yet, announcing in big letters: 'Noël Coward's *Private Lives*. Don't miss it!'

Tanner set up the table and Henry, having decided to dispense with the soda, took a shot from the bottle, which he offered to Tanner.

'Is there never any music in this place? Or have my ears gone as well?' Henry made his way across the room to the doorway where he bellowed, 'Ahmed, *Ahmed*. Music, man, where's the music?'

There was a muttered reply from the waiter who vanished behind the counter and a moment later the strains of James Last filtered through the speakers on the wall. Henry aimed his cue and neatly split the pack with a deft shot.

'This won't do,' he muttered and went back to yell at the bewildered Ahmed.

'Not this rubbish, lavatory music. You know what I want.'

The record was duly changed for the wailing lute of a local Arabic singer, and they returned to their game.

'I hear you had some bad luck on your last trip,' said Henry. Tanner related the accident with the truck.

'You can't blame yourself for that kind of thing. What did that toad Thompson have to say about it?'

'They're trying to play it down, keep it quiet.'

Henry laughed, and then cursed himself for missing a pocket.

'You can't keep anything quiet in this town. The papers don't report anything, you see, which makes people talk even more. There are no secrets – well, there are, it's just that everyone knows them.'

'I'm going south in a few days,' said Tanner, trying to catch up Henry's lead.

'What the hell are you going down there for? There's a war on as far as I can recall.'

'Well, I'm hoping to avoid that. I won't be down there long.'

The sound of applause came from the makeshift theatre on the lawn outside. Henry put his cue down.

'That's it, they're all loose again. Time to go, I think, before they all flood in here to discuss the damn thing.'

'I probably won't see you before I go.'

'Well, make sure you come back then. There's far too few people I can still have a maudlin conversation with as it is.'

'We'll have a drink when I get back.'

'Do you know,' Henry said suddenly, 'they stopped me the other night?'

'Who?'

'The damn police, they pulled me over. Fair enough it was a little late.'

Tanner shook his head in mock disapproval. 'That's what the curfew is for, to warn people like you to stay at home.'

'They were going to flog me, flog me with a leather whip like a common criminal for having a drink.'

'That's what the law says.'

'But that's the whole point. It's not law, it's bloody religion, and it's not my religion anyway, just as it's not half the bloody

73

country's religion. You can't just start flogging people and chopping their hands off.' He dismissed the case with a wave of his hand. 'It won't last, you wait and see. It can't possibly last.'

A crowd entered the lounge bar and more people could be seen coming up the steps to the veranda. A voice called out to Henry, and a woman in her forties swept across in a brightly coloured *djellabia* with huge amber beads hanging from her neck.

'Henry, what a surprise.' She glanced at Tanner and smiled. 'Who's your friend?' she asked, raising her eyebrows.

'Just a friend, I'm afraid,' Henry replied, raising his shoulders in regret towards Tanner, saying, 'too late, I'm afraid, the jackals are upon us.'

Tanner smiled and walked towards the door. 'I must be going anyway.'

'Have a safe trip then, and remember what I said,' called Henry in parting before the woman demanded his attention again.

'Henry, you do talk in riddles sometimes.'

Tanner wandered through the crowds and found his way out of the haze of whisky and laughing, talking people.

The following morning Tanner went to see Thompson about the trip south. He parked the car in the next road against the wall of the office. A battery of four large metal air-cooler units protruded from the wall. Little beggar children, hobos of the backstreets, sat in the shade under the units. Water ran through straw pads through which the air was sucked and pumped into the building. The children would poke their fingers through the grille to feel the water, careful not to push through too far into the sharp blades of the fan. Sometimes they'd just press against the underside of the metal boxes where it was cool and dark. In the afternoon they'd sleep under the coolers.

The office was busy today, full of noise and bustle: telephones ringing, typewriters clicking away furiously. Red lights came on in the ceiling when an international line was open, so that everyone could get their calls through. Waiting for lines could go on for days. There was a general swirl of movement and noise, everyone looking busy, telex machines clattering into life of their own accord. A man with a cloth wrapped round his head circulated with a tray of glasses, replacing empty ones with fresh ones brimful with steaming, hot, sweet, red tea. Above the vague hum of efficiency there was the sound of raised voices in consultation or conversation, a swift jibe or a long rambling monotone.

Thompson was reading a letter when Tanner entered the office.

'Ah, just the man, sit down.' He indicated the chair and slipped the letter into his top pocket. Tanner looked a mess. He wanted to ask him to have a haircut and a good shave.

'Our friend has arrived at last, it seems.'

'The American?'

'Yes, Mr . . .' Thompson consulted a letter on his desk, 'Gilmour, Mr Charles Gilmour. He's here already.'

'When are we going down there?'

'As soon as possible, really.'

The phone rang and Thompson raised a hand to halt Tanner's next question. Tanner sat back in his chair and looked round at the set of curled-up posters stuck to the panelled walls. The pictures depicted scenes from the field: smiling workers round a drill section, a man in a hard hat examining gauges on a rig, two men looking up from a map spread out on the hood of a Land Rover; all wore spotless clothes. The pictures looked like they'd been taken about ten years ago. The sky was the wrong shade of blue. Thompson's one-sided conversation was going on in the background.

'Sayed, what can I say? Of course we will.'

Long slow laughter, like a dying hyena.

'No, no, no as soon as we can, of course, we must get together again.' A pause as he listened, the laugh beginning again, then stopping.

'No, we'll definitely have the papers for you, yes, yes.'

The conversation came to an end and Thompson put the phone down and cleared his throat.

'Now where were we?'

'He's here already, you were saying,' reminded Tanner.

'That's right.' Thompson pushed the strands of hair back across his head.

'Tonight, can you pick him up at the Hilton? There's a party at the Hansens'.'

He paused mid-sentence. 'You know the Hansens, don't you?'

Tanner knew them vaguely; they had met once or twice. Hansen was Swedish or something. The idea of having to socialise with the visiting dignitary had not occurred to him.

'Seven at the Hilton. I'd do it myself but I have another engagement.'

The two men sat face to face. Tanner wanted to ask if it was really necessary for him to be involved in this social event. Thompson smiled as if the matter was already decided.

In the room down the hall the noise had not abated. Hamdi was negotiating a deal on black-market dollars to buy spare parts. The only way to do business was to purchase hard currency on a black market which was flourishing.

The desk opposite where Tanner sat was empty; Suliman's mother had died and he was away in mourning.

Outside in the tranquil garden an old man wandered barefoot on the grass, draping hosepipe and sprinkler across the lawn. Tanner walked quietly down the drive, away from the mayhem.

TEN

It was just after seven when Tanner pushed through the silver doors of the Hilton Hotel. The marble floor gleamed a cool dark green under the light from a huge elaborate chandelier which hung over the entrance lobby. Here bell-boys dressed in awkward-fitting red monkey suits moved about tight-chested as they ushered guests from door to desk and desk to lift and lift to roundabout revolving door. Well-to-do locals came here in their best Savile Row suits and frocks from Harrods. They came to mingle and be seen in lavish disposition, surrounded by the more casually dressed visitors from abroad, who lounged in open-necked shirts and jeans around the Piano Bar to sip alcohol-free Tropical Fruit Punch. Later they would move to the restaurant for a three-course meal of extravagance.

Tanner crossed the lobby to the front desk and leaned on it. There was a certain amount of urgency in the activity behind the desk. An Egyptian-looking man, pale skin and a thin moustache, located the room number for Tanner and handed him the receiver while conducting a conversation with a guest who had lost his luggage at the airport three hours ago.

A voice answered the phone.

'Mr Gilmour? My name's Tanner. I believe Geoffrey Thompson called to say he couldn't make it.'

Gilmour said he'd be right down. Tanner waited by the desk, watching the people come and go, thinking about the voice of the man he'd just spoken to. There was a guarded note to it, as though he were holding something back.

The Egyptian desk clerk rested his elbow on the counter and pointed behind Tanner with his pencil. Tanner looked in surprise at the man who was being indicated, then he stepped forward and reached out a hand to meet the offered paw.

'Mr Tanner, I presume,' said the tall black man with a wry grin.

Gilmour carried his large frame with an upright confidence. He was dressed in an immaculate light grey tropical suit with an open-necked shirt and soft brown leather casuals on his feet. The thick-banded watch on his left wrist looked heavy and expensive. The fact that Gilmour was a black man came as something of a surprise to Tanner, who nevertheless found it quite amusing. He wondered if Thompson was aware of the fact. It seemed likely to Tanner that he had absolutely no idea. The big man gripped Tanner's hand in his huge powerful grasp. He was about six inches taller than Tanner.

The two doormen, dressed in purple, each held a door open, never breaking the flow of their own conversation as the guests passed in and out. Tanner led the way towards his parked car. He straightened his shirt and wondered if perhaps he should have changed it. They made conversation about flights and time differences. The American reminded Tanner of a heavyweight boxer on the verge of retirement. It was hard to put an age to him though Tanner guessed he must be around the fifty mark. The car seemed small and cramped now, but if Gilmour was in any discomfort he never mentioned it.

'Where are you from, Tanner?' he asked as his host wrestled the gearstick into place. Tanner almost laughed out loud at the suddenness of such a forward question. He began to explain as they drove slowly down through the hotel driveway with its trimmed bougainvillaea and subtle lighting.

The wind seemed to be picking up; the night air was comfortable and cool, a world away from the air-conditioned lobby they had just left which seemed almost too cold. During the day it was a relief to step through the glass doors out of the inferno and feel the sweat stop dead half-way down your back. From inside the walls of this oasis of polished steel and glass the outside world could be viewed with more rational detachment. It was possible to breathe in here. From the road the hotel was lit up like a shrine; you could see it shining from the other side of the river. A candle in the darkness of the surrounding fields and abandoned land.

The dual carriageway ran along the river front, guiding the way for people who lived across the concrete bridge in the third town of the trio. Omdurman was the old town where the Mahdi and his Companions of the Prophet had sat and planned their conquest of the Islamic world.

Now it was evening, and the people were coming to see the big bright shops and the lights of the city, rattling past in overladen buses and taxis, sweating in the night air while the driver cursed and kicked his way through the snarling traffic. Did they have a moment as they rushed by to glance up at this colossal monolithic sideshow? Did they wonder for a moment what it might be like to stay there for a night or eat a meal there in the restaurants, or did they care at all? Did they see the shuffling figure of a homeless child who crouched in the glare of their headlights and waited for a lull in the stream so that he might launch out across the road and vanish into the shadows by the river looking for somewhere to shelter for the night? Did they see any of it at all? Perhaps they just stared out the car window trying to ignore the armpit of the person next to them into which they were crammed. Maybe the lights of the big hotel were a welcome view to take their minds off whatever they had left behind them tonight, or wherever they were to return to that night. Craning their necks for one last glimpse before it was all swallowed by the trees and the bend in the river and the dark street lamps that hung over the road like vultures. A relief perhaps from the picture of the boy with straight hair and shiny teeth who looked like no child of theirs, who filled the advertising board looking up at the big hotel. He had always looked at the hotel; even before it was built the boy in the toothpaste advertisement had always looked up at it. Then the floodlit walls and the flags that whipped in the night air would be gone until the next time they came by.

The dual carriageway had never been properly finished, said Tanner in an attempt to explain. There were sections where the breeze-blocks had been dropped in the dirt next to each other, waiting for someone else to come along and arrange them in a line.

They still waited in piles which just collected dust. People used them as seats while they waited for a bus to turn up with enough room left for them to squeeze on to.

Tanner followed the road that led past all the old hotels, each representing a time gone by. Each in its day had been the place to stay, the premier spot to be seen in, the height of luxury and splendour. The Grand Hotel, with its weary tables and wicker chairs that stood neglected on the veranda under the huge dusty palms. The tired paintwork and deserted lobbies gave it a forlorn peaceful look. Once it had been the diamond of this tree-lined section of the river, just down from the presidential palace with some of the best views of the river from the big louvre windows and balconies. Built into the surroundings it was a relic of a bygone architecture.

The headlights of the oncoming cars flashed and dazzled on the dark road where no streetlights worked and no illumination came from the faded hotels. The road carried on past the government buildings and army barracks, through the neon white palace. The lights from Khartoum North were like pinprick flames that licked across the surface of the gentle undulation of sleeping water. The worn-out river bank clung to its source of life under the heavy swaying branches which hung down in subordinate respect.

They turned off the river road and cut through the centre of town. Tanner was wondering if the reality was anything like Gilmour had been expecting. To his surprise Gilmour went on to say that it wasn't that different to what he had expected and indeed some aspects reminded him of a trip to Mexico that he'd made some years ago.

'Somewhere down in the sleepy South, it seems.'

'Which part of the States are you from, then?'

'The north, Washington DC – well, Seattle really.'

'I've never been there,' said Tanner, trying to make idle conversation though he was well aware how obvious it was. He was not looking forward to this evening at all.

'Well, you should go one day – it's worth a look. Big place though,' Gilmour replied.

'So you enjoy travelling then, do you?'

'Well, I don't get that much in this job, but yes I do like to get away, see new places and meet new faces.' Gilmour paused to look out the window as they passed a Shell station. Nodding at it, he said, 'Some things aren't all that different around the world – some things don't change at all.'

Tanner wanted to ask him why they had sent him in particular but felt perhaps Gilmour was getting bored now with this conversation. They carried on through town, and Gilmour remained silent.

They passed a barricaded wall. Tanner couldn't remember what it was that was barricaded; it might have been a hostel for the Amul, the secret police. There was a dark gash in the pale concrete. Three armed soldiers leaned back against the wall on rickety metal chairs, black gleaming metal resting in their laps. They were smoking and laughing, paying no attention to the passing cars. Rubbish lined the street, piled high in places. There was a scrawny wild cat sitting right on the top of one heap watching the cars and the people pass by. A gaudy pink striplight indicated a tin shack with grapefruit piled on the raised counter, electric liquidisers racked alongside, customers standing around in the dim eerie gloom sipping cold sweet drinks. Two tall thin figures caught in the headlights moved along to the side, ambling along in the shadows. Too tall to be northerners, they would be from the West or the South, probably from the South. They'd come attracted by the glitter of these same gaudy pink lights that advertised the cold drink stand. During the day plagues of flies would hover and dart around the same lights in a frenzy over the sickly sweet smell from the fruit. They would find their way round to the rear of the shack where the discarded peel would be thrown to rot. Like the flies, the people came, travelling for days in the back of lorries, attracted by the silver spoon of wealth that they couldn't understand. There was something here that would be good for them, and they wanted a taste of it. They found work quite often on the building sites through a friend or a relative, or simply through their own perseverance. As they were unskilled they would be given instructions by a northerner. They were treated like animals and they were probably paid less; but there was little opportunity for other work so they buckled down, took the insults and accepted the meagre pay. They lived in shanty towns, cardboard huts held together with bits of string and rusty wire. They lived there with their wives and kids, a stone's throw from the big painted houses that had been built if not by them then by their predecessors. There were new arrivals every day, stumbling in from the desert in a swirl of dust-storm thirst, only to find that this oasis of electric promises was running out of excuses; soon the mirage would be returning to sand and light.

The roads were laid out in the pattern of a Union Jack centred on the palace. Straight lines cut into the shapeless sand, but with time this stone skeleton outline was being eroded, sharp corners were rounded; another sign that this was a place that could not survive without a struggle. Left alone, the elements of nature would follow their course, and their scheme of things did not include the automobiles, the coloured lights or the air-conditioning, it did not include man and all the paraphernalia that accompanies that folly. For man to remain here as he was now would require him to fight; he must fight for what he had come to represent and more importantly for what he had come to need. The fight to sustain life had to be fought every day of the year, and this was where it was so obvious that man was failing. He had overstepped himself, this was clear; what would once have been sufficient was no longer so. The years of neglect were making themselves known. They demanded attention, now.

The party was at the Hansens' house, in honour of Mrs Hansen's birthday. Mr Hansen worked for the company and it seemed a good opportunity, Thompson had said, to make Gilmour feel at ease. The fact that Thompson himself would not be attending made Tanner even more reluctant to go along.

They pulled up outside and Tanner led the way, holding the wide iron gate open for Gilmour. As they walked through the overgrown garden Tanner could make out the voice of Hansen in a bellow of laughter that rolled through the house and out to the garden. Eric Hansen was a small man, somewhat shorter than his

82

wife who was also about ten years younger than his mid-fifties. He had a habit of laughing at his own jokes which nobody ever seemed to understand. Some said this was due to his English not being very good, or else the Scandinavian sense of humour.

The house was empty, all the windows and doors flung wide open to let the night and the guests pass through freely. The guests were assembled in the garden at the back, scattered round a small table covered in bottles and glasses. The rear garden was a little more spacious, the lawn uncluttered and neatly clipped.

Mr Hansen leapt to his feet and came across the lawn to greet them, stroking the beer from his walrus moustache.

'Welcome, welcome, please.' He pumped Tanner's hand furiously and clapped him on the back. Tanner made the introduction. Hansen shook hands with Gilmour.

'Eric, please call me Eric.' He led them back to the table where this evening's guests were now assembled. They were a cross section of expatriate society: a German couple, a Coptic merchant, an Englishman from the visa section of the British Embassy and two engineers and their wives who were all English. There was a Sudanese man who was something in the University and his Polish wife.

They sat down and Hansen poured them each a foaming glass of his homemade beer. Mrs Hansen came out of the house behind them wearing a gaudy *djellabia* and a pair of spectacles that put Tanner in mind of Nana Mouskouri. She was escorting the final guest across the garden. The girl was in her mid-twenties, an English journalist who had recently returned from a trip to the South in search of a story.

The evening progress with the sound of conversation growing louder and Hansen going to and from the house, returning each time with a fresh jug of his homebrew. Mrs Hansen moved round the guests with dishes of open sandwiches. Tanner found that luckily Gilmour was good at socialising, engaging everyone at the table in conversation in rotation, talking about everything and anything; he seemed to be quite a knowledgeable man. Tanner was listening to the journalist girl who was talking about her journey. She had flown to Juba with the intention of making her way back overland. Things had gone seriously wrong, though. She fell ill with dysentery and spent three weeks in the back of a truck which brought her most of the way back. For the last stretch from El Fula she took a train. She was still not fully recovered and disappeared into the house at frequent intervals.

'Stupid bloody thing to do anyway,' muttered one of the engineers during one of her absences.

'Why?' asked Tanner. 'Because she went on her own?'

'Because she went at all,' said the engineer.

'She says she wanted to find out what was going on.'

The engineer waved a hand dismissively. 'It's a bloody war zone, there's a war going on. Leave 'em to it is what I say, it's not our business to interfere.' He went on, levelling a finger at Tanner, 'It's your people who should be down there finding out what's going on, not young girls like her.'

The girl in question was making her way across the lawn back to the table. A hush fell over the group for a moment.

'I think it's really awful, all this violence and things,' said Mrs Hansen. 'Really, I mean I heard the other day about a priest.' She paused to think for a second. 'He was a Jesuit priest, I believe, anyway they kidnapped this old man, these rebel soldiers, an old man, he must have been about eighty-five, I think. They kept him prisoner for – I don't know – three months? Then finally they released him and he had to walk two hundred miles to get to a town or something. I mean, can you imagine, to hundred miles he walked?'

'So they let him go unharmed then?' asked the journalist girl, pulling out a notebook from her handbag.

'Oh yes,' confirmed Mrs Hansen, shaking the bracelets on her wrist as she wagged her finger at the air. 'You see no one was going to pay for him. He was a teacher in a school but the government didn't want to pay, and the church said they couldn't afford it.'

'Because he was an old man and no one cared what happened to him.'

'I don't know whether it is always as simple as that,' interjected Gilmour with a small trace of a smile appearing on his face. 'These things can be just as hard to deal with in practical terms as any other.'

The trees round the back garden were beginning to bend in the increasing blow of the wind. A plastic beaker blew over on the table.

'Oh dear,' said Mrs Hansen. 'I think it might rain.'

'No, not rain I don't think,' said the learned Sudanese gentleman who was trying to start his pipe.

'How do you know it's not rain?' asked Mrs Hansen with a note of mock indignation in her voice.

'You can smell rain – you can always smell it before it arrives,' said Tanner.

'That's true,' said Hansen gathering up his jug again. 'This is just a bit of wind.' He laughed.

'But I think we should move inside, dear,' said Mrs Hansen.

The dust storm arrived in minutes; the garden was alive with the sting of whirling sand. The guests made their way into the house, carrying what they could salvage from the table. Inside the house Mrs Hansen was running frantically from door to window in an attempt to shut the house to the storm. Already the dust was blowing in the living-room, making everyone cough; it was hard to breathe. Finally the shutters were closed and the windows bolted. Everyone was covered in dirt and the chairs and tables in a thin film of fine dust. Mrs Hansen was being consoled by her husband – she had fallen on the steps in her haste to get the doors closed. She sat and rubbed her knee.

'I don't fancy driving in this,' said one engineer.

'No, no,' said Hansen, waving his hand at no one in particular. 'You must all stay here until it clears. You can't drive in this weather.'

The guests settled down and Hansen managed to find some clean glasses and another jug of beer. The sound of the thrashing trees and the dust scouring at the shutters was a distant roar. The conversation turned back to the state of the country, and the rumours that things were coming to a head; it would get worse before it got better. Despite the fact that rumours waned in reliability as they circled and grew in stature, there was still an

85

edge of truth somewhere within. There were rumours of rebel armies rising in the South and the West of the country, beyond the confines of the claustrophobia of the three towns. Something was stirring out in the darkness, rising in a tide that might sweep the country before it.

There were rumours in the city of the number of hangings and floggings that went on, tributes to the triumph of barbarism over reason. In the face of opposition the force of law was returning to shelter under the skirts of religion, so that perhaps the fear of God might somehow assist them in alleviating distrust and unrest.

The horrific grip had so entranced the people that they flocked enthralled to be witnesses to these public affairs, like ardent fans to a football match. Perhaps like the citizens of Pompeii, turning their backs on the volcano to watch the savagery of the arena.

A state of siege was in operation. The tales spelt out the dire measures being taken by a regime hemmed in on all fronts. The power of the police was being handed out to an increasingly unaccountable force. The secret police was expanding all the time; fervent young men armed and given free rein had frightening echoes in the pages of history.

In the arrests that took place daily, in the silent curfew streets, in the suppressed rumours of famine and the tales of the toll of war: in all of these there was a current of suspense; events were moving relentlessly towards the brink, beyond which change must lie. In the land of forgotten dreams, anticipation was infectious. Salvation must surely be just around the corner.

The party was starting to break up as in twos and threes the guests began to brave the storm, which was now slackening off.

Tanner asked Gilmour if he was ready to go.

'So soon? We only just got here.'

Tanner began to explain about the curfew, but Gilmour laughed. 'No, I was only joking, son. Sure, let's go.'

The American then went round saying his goodbyes. Mrs Hansen led him to the door, saying to Tanner, 'Thank you for coming along, and for bringing our American friend, he's great.' Tanner looked out to the garden where Gilmour was already at the gate.

'Yes,' he agreed. 'He seems to be one of those people who are at ease anywhere.' He smiled amiably.

When he got to the car Gilmour was already inside waiting patiently to be driven off.

'You never lock your car here – is the crime rate so low?' he asked.

'Well,' said Tanner, fumbling in his pockets for the keys,' I don't think there's anything worth stealing in it. Besides, that window is broken.'

Tanner started the car and drove carefully through the streets. There was a change recognisable in Gilmour that had struck Tanner as soon as he got in the car.

'I hope that I'm not going to spend weeks here being paraded round the social scene.'

'I thought you enjoyed yourself.'

'I am here to work. I need to get into the field. I don't see the point in delaying the departure any longer than is necessary.'

Tanner looked across at the American, but in the dim light of the car he could just see a man staring straight ahead into the headlights of the oncoming cars.

ELEVEN

The following night Tanner drove across the river to an unfamiliar part of the town. He had spent the evening at Caesar's place with the moon-eyed girl. Now he was driving through the dwindling late-night streets away from his home. He had done this before; he enjoyed exploring the small lanes and the anonymous faces of the people there. Sometimes he caught a taxi and just climbed out when something caught his eye, like a street corner or the lights of a café or the wrought-iron pattern on somebody's front gate.

In the early evening you could wander through the crowds gathered outside the cinemas. Under the huge high walls brightly lit and gaudy from neglect, tatters of faded colourful posters advertised a show from some time ago: larger-than-life paintings of guns and exploding flame and square-cut heroes and glamorous heroines advertising sex. The titles were meaningless – they could be in any number of languages, English, Arabic, Hindi or even Italian and occasionally French. No one seemed to care much about what was said, so long as there was enough action and plenty of women to jeer at. Some of the crowd had no intention of seeing the film; they may even have seen the picture earlier in the week. They just stood outside and talked all night, the sounds of the film creeping over the walls from inside in a blurr of threats and promises.

The vendors stood around selling their peanuts and roasted melon seeds, calling to each other across the heads of the crowd. Through the dusty squares of light people wandered in and out, pausing to greet a friend or a relative. Cars drove by, taxis lurched into the kerb and away again, exchanging one load for another, the driver pressing one hand firmly to the horn and with the other holding the gearstick in place. There were all kinds of people here, some dressed in their best shirts, batwing collars and flared trousers. Others with battered slippers hanging off the back of the feet, dirty white shapeless *djellabias* hanging off one shoulder where a seam had gone. Long uneven hair full of dust and strands of cotton, picked at slowly with the long teeth of a wooden comb. The opportunists were here also, slipping through the crowds with delight, deft fingers looking for easy pickings.

Tanner walked on past the carnival masses and the jagged neon burlesque, away from the vivid intrusion, continuing towards the dimly lit side streets that led secretly back to anonymity. Behind him he could feel the flurry of life, the explosion of noise and sound and light, waning with every step that he took. The collision of so many lives scared him. It exuded an odour of contorted suffering concealed and he did not wish to inhale it. The gloomy light from an intermittent street lamp slipped its arm around his shoulders in a comforting embrace that was almost illicit. It was here that he felt he belonged, fleeing through the back streets between the regret and the discarded misery of other people's lives. His footsteps started a dog that was nosing through a pile of rubbish. With a muffled cry and a glance from the mournful eyes of a well-kicked dog, the scavenger took off with its tail between its legs. Further on, a girl cleared her throat and stepped into an inert pool of light. Tanner dropped his eyes and hurried on without looking at her.

He passed a tea shop that was closing down for the night. The metal doors clamped shut with a bolt that snapped across. People were disappearing into the shadows with a last word cast over departing shoulders. It was getting towards curfew time. He turned to see which way led back to the car. He hurried now, back through the same streets. No one around, and the shadows seemed to have taken on a new, more menacing, edge.

Across the square, which had been packed with people the last time he'd walked by. How long had he been walking? An hour, or was it more? Scraps of newspaper, peanut shells, half-eaten pastries ground into the dust. Footprints criss-crossed and obliterated each other on the ground. He found the car alone on the street. A taxi rolled by filled with people and listing badly to one side. Here there were still a few people about. The car started and he drove through the streets and back towards the bridge. He was annoyed with himself for having lost track of the time. He struck the wheel and turned on to the bridge. The soldiers were pulling the barricades across. The soldier hesitated, hitched up his too short trousers and with one hand and waved Tanner by with his rifle.

On the other side there was no one in sight. He sped through the deserted city, cursing himself for having left it so late. He tried to work out the best way home, and turned to go round behind the airport. He was about two miles from home when the car coughed to a halt. Just across the street was a petrol station, closed of course. He locked the car and began to walk, cutting away from the road in the shortest line towards the lights of his street that twinkled across the open darkness in between. It was a cool night and the air felt fresh. He began to relax as he walked. He was safe out here in the middle of nowhere. He turned to look back and the car was a dark metallic shadow in the moonlight. It seemed small and a long way off. He didn't really mind the inconvenience of having run out of petrol. He didn't even mind the fact that he was outside so late. The element of danger seemed to excite him – he felt full of energy suddenly, as though he wanted to shout or sing at the top of his voice; he felt a sense of elation.

He was about three hundred metres from the road ahead when he heard a car. Then he saw it, the headlights bringing it along fast. He looked again and there was a man on the road now. A man standing in the path of the speeding car. He saw the figure raise its arms in the direction of the car. There was no change in the car's speed. The soldier fired and the shots echoed away into the night sky. Tanner had not moved. He stood completely still, mesmerised by this sudden asphyxiating change in the air. The car crashed to a halt, turning half way around so that the headlights pointed back the way it had come. The windscreen was now an empty frame lined with fragments that glittered like a handful of stars caught in a net. There was a sound that was long and thin, unbroken screaming. The soldiers – there were four or five of them

90

now – appearing as though summoned silently from the shadows. Voices, shouts, harsh and unforgiving.

Tanner walked away, further down the road, still in the dust. He walked until he could only just see the headlights as pinpricks in the darkness before he crossed the road and ran towards the buildings and the streets, the walls of his house.

The following day being Friday, the offices were closed. It was early afternoon by the time Tanner had the Fiat running again.

He coaxed the car over the railway tracks. He turned left and followed the road that led past the sidings and the big rusty buffers which marked the end of the line. Twisted iron and weeds gathered here. The wreckage of old discarded railcars, burnt-out shells of carriages that had colllapsed and rested now on their sides, motionless. The graveyard where these dead beasts lay as a reminder of an age gone by, and of all the thousands of miles that led off into the dusty tracks, was now a playground for the small children who came from the houses nearby. The collection of houses – conical huts – was built years ago by the rail board for the brake men and the engine drivers, so their families had somewhere to wait for them.

The steam trains still ran though some of the boilers were over fifty years old. The service was slow and erratic at the best of times. The lines were subject to the seasons: they were washed out quite regularly in the rainy season, bringing the single-track system to a standstill. The trains would roll to a halt and sit and wait for the sun to evaporate the barrier away, often miles from anywhere, right in the middle of an empty nowhere. The passangers would get off and wander about trying to find somewhere cool to rest until the train resumed its journey.

The compounds in front of the houses were marked out in bamboo and chicken wire, through which long-eared goats poked their heads and scavenged in the ground for anything edible, chewing contentedly all the time.

Across the tracks from the railway houses was a different class of home. A row of high brick walls with flat roofs and hidden gardens over which the tip of a luxuriant tree was the only indication of the splendour lying within. The walls were all painted in greys or white with the occasional yellow or even pink thrown in. A few had been left unplastered for some reason – perhaps the work had been abandoned at some stage when the owner ran out of cash.

Tanner pulled up outside a tall black-painted gate, decorated with birds flying and galleons sailing, all in wrought-iron and metalwork.

The door was hot to the touch and he knocked loudly. The gate creaked open and a young boy of about thirteen stood to one side and invited Tanner in, shaking hands politely. The garden was not large but it was well tended, bougainvillaea blossoms splashing the pale green foliage with pink. Tanner walked along the paving stones that marked out the path through the garden. From within the dark interior of the main building a voice called across the veranda. Tanner shouted a greeting in reply and in turn a long deep laugh came from inside. Tanner reached the veranda and stepped up into the shade. He was met by a tall wide-boned man with a mess of short grey curls on his head. Though he was old now, his body racked with arthritis, it was obvious from the way he walked and from his hands, which gripped Tanner's now that he had once been a powerful figure of a man. He used to be a merchant sailor – that was his trade and his profession for thirty-eight years: his life. His hands with their strong sinewy fingers were gnarled and scarred from the work. On his left arm he carried a long scar that measured seven and a half inches, the result of a knife fight that took place in one port or another – the exact location seemed to vary each time he told the story. Just above the scar was a tattoo depicting an arrow and a bird in flight, both eclipsed by a crescent moon.

Hammoudi El Tayyb was the only name Tanner had known when he had arrived for the first time in Khartoum three years ago, the old friend of his father's. When Tanner had written explaining that he was coming out, and that he would like to try to find work for a while, Hammoudi wrote back saying that he was very welcome to stay at his house. In fact, within a month of his arrival he had pulled some strings with a relative who worked in a small oil company that was just setting up an office in town. Tanner took the job gratefully, and though he was welcome to stay on with El Tayyb and his wife, her sister and their son Salim, he decided to move out into a place of his own. Hammoudi had given him a doorway into a country and a culture that was totally alien to him.

Hammoudi was full of long-drawn-out anecdotes about the years he had spent in the navy, often bringing Tanner's father into the story – sometimes, thought Tanner, for his benefit. He used to be a regular visitor to Hammoudi's house, but recently he'd been so wrapped up in his own problems that he'd been putting off coming to see him.

Today they sat on the veranda and the boy Salim brought out a tray with a jug of iced fresh lemonade. The old man slipped his crocodile-skin slippers off his feet and scratched his big toe. Tanner handed over his gift. The old man opened the cardboard box and removed the piece of pink coral that Tanner had brought back with him from the Red Sea. Hammoudi El Tayyb smiled to himself when he saw it, rubbing his thumb over the sharp rough surface, gently stroking it. They sat back and more refreshment was brought while Hammoudi began to describe what was going on in his household. He talked about his son and how he was working hard at school. He wanted his son to do well; he needed to get very high marks to qualify for the University. The competition was fierce and though he was still a good five years away from the qualifying exams, his father was taking no chances on his son not succeeding. While Hammoudi talked on, Tanner, though envying that single-minded purpose, felt his thoughts drifting. He began to think about what would happen if Nina became pregnant. They had not invested sufficiently in each other to make the idea of bringing a child into the world possible.

The old man turned away from the station and the wind caught the tear that rolled down his cheek, sending his sorrow off on wings of dusty shame. He walked steadily through the crowds of misery. The small town lay on the borders of the open west: Kabbabish land. The outskirts were flooded with

93

refugees. The policemen in Khaki outfits wielded long whips and drove the crowds back – though back to where? This was a tide that could not be turned. He had to move quickly to avoid being caught in the mêlée.

He didn't turn to look behind him; he knew what the outcome would be: the crowds would be pushed backwards inch by inch. He had to wonder at these people. Their leaders, the sheikhs and the nazirs, the head men, they said that the government would take care of their needs. All they had to do was to make their way to the big towns where the government was, then their plight could not be ignored. The old man had never been to the capital of his country; it was another world to him. What could they tell him about his sheep and goats, from their little offices and their pieces of paper? How did these sheikhs know that they would receive any help? Did they even know the rains had failed again, or was the fact just put away somewhere, in a box marked 'Starvation'?

But the times were changing, and even as the old man made his way through the urgent crowd he knew that his way of life had changed for ever. Maybe the rains would come finally, but the flock was lost and that could not be reversed. They were out in the desert sun, turning to dust. It had been impossible to move them any further. They had only just made it back with the family. The two camels that remained were overloaded to breaking point. Each and every step they took was an answer to a prayer, each jolting metre was in doubt.

There was no more to it. Their prayers had been answered and they had made it out of the desert and into this place of human desolation.

His place was the desert, the only place he knew. Back through time to his father, and his father before him, the roots were deep and wide. It was his turn to play out his role in the story of things. The role that lay before him was that of the final act. The last figure in the landscape. Behind him the door would be closed for ever.

His tears came freely now. All the family that he had ever known, his wife, her sister and her husband, his daughter and all the children. All of them were huddled together now, waiting for a decision to be made that would grant them life or condemn them to slow death.

'Let us take our case to them, brothers, let us show them that we are truly in need and deserving of their help. They have food, they will give to us.'

Perhaps they would, but he had heard someone say that there was no mention of their plight on the wireless. No mention? No, the government had enough of their own problems to deal with. But there was no doubt in his mind that this was the only place for the children. There was nothing else he could do, they had a chance here of surviving, perhaps. The future would then be safe in their hands. He kissed the child that his daughter had held in her arms.

He reached the camels where he had left them, by the old well. He looked round, remembering this place in his youth, when the men from the other families would turn up; you never knew who you might meet here. Some of the best and some of the worst men you could hope to meet, but he loved them all. The well was dry.

He stopped dead in his tracks when he saw the young boy who sat in the shade of the gnarled tree. The boy looked up and waved a hand in greeting. The boy had been picked up on the way back; he was lost, and his family had been killed in a camel raid by armed marauders. The boy stood up and held out a sack of water that he had got from somewhere. The old man shook his head in gratitude. Then he picked up the halter, and clicked a command at the camel that sat on the ground next to the boy. The camel struggled to its feet and the old man hung the waterbag across the saddle. Then he turned and began to walk into the desert.

After a few moments the old man stopped and turned, to see that the boy was to his surprise walking some way behind him. He thought for a moment then waved to the boy, and sprinted the yards between them and stood before him.

They turned together, the old man and the young boy. They walked into the north-west; on a map the direction they were headed for led to a section that formed a perfect right angle, a corner; an empty quarter. They moved out into the thorn bushes and the hard flat ground, into the very heat-haze itself. A layer of pure heat swam over the ground like a wave, which soon swallowed the two figures, the hard outlines melting into the swaying landscape.

SOUTH

TWELVE

The shadow of the small plane twisted and jerked across the rivers and the trees as it hugged the open ground and the sand and stones. Like the wings of a dark angel through the furnace landscape, the plane moved relentlessly south.

Crouched in the almost bucket-like seat, Tanner looked forward from the back of the plane to where Gilmour was speaking to the pilot. He wondered what they were talking about. They each had headphones on, but it was impossible to make out the words above the noise of the engines. Tanner stared out of the small window on his left through the blur of propellers to the soft brown below. They'd been in the air for over an hour now. Tanner wanted to get up and go for a walk. He was unable even to stretch out his legs.

There was a gradual change in the ground. The towns faded away and so did the houses and roads. For a while they flew above the main road to Medani before turning off and peeling away. The plane climbed steadily. Below, the green of the Gezira cotton scheme was oddly out of place in the landscape. There was a crop sprayer cutting low across the fields.

The pilot was an Australian working for the air taxi service, a large taciturn man who gazed indifferently through the windshield. Tanner wondered again what the two men were talking about. Below them the river was a silver thread which was lost again as they turned away west. The ground became silent. The twin-engined Cessna was a white spectre from the ground; a bead of mercury rolling across the sky. Tanner closed his eyes and tried to sleep.

When he woke up they were banking tightly over the field station, with its dusty white tents and a pair of what looked like rectangular Portakabins. There was a small adobe mud building in one corner beside a large tree. There was no sign of anyone. The plane dropped in a slow curve, the pilot tight-lipped gripping the steering column. They made one final low sweep and then they were brushing the tree tops and skimming into the landing strip which opened out suddenly before them, a long flat plain that had been stripped of all the bushes and rocks that would have been obstacles. The line was marked out with small tattered white flags.

The wheels bounced once, then they were running along the ground. They came to a halt. Spooner, the pilot, flicked the switches and the engines stopped. Tanner climbed out behind Gilmour and dropped off the wing to join him. There was no sign of anyone in any direction. It was almost nightfall, the sun rapidly sinking towards the cold horizon, turning the world orange.

'Doesn't seem to be anybody around,' said Spooner.

'No,' agreed Tanner. 'It seems pretty quiet.'

'Have you been here before?' Gilmour asked the pilot, who shook his head.

'And you haven't either?' he said, looking at Tanner, who also shook his head.

They stood for a minute or two, staring at the sun. Spooner was busy doing things to the plane.

'Are you going back tonight?' Tanner asked him.

Spooner straightened up from under the wing and wiped his hands with a rag. He shook his head. 'If I'm going to get back, I got to go now, right away.'

Tanner nodded and turned to Gilmour. 'There must be someone over there. I'll go and see what I can find.'

Spooner tossed the rag into the plane and fished in his pocket for a cigarette.

'I'll wait till you get back then, but try and be as quick as possible. I don't want to have to stay out here tonight unless I have to.'

Tanner said he would, then he walked quickly through the fluttering markers and across the plain. It took only a minute or

100

two to get into the area of the station. Nothing was moving, and he walked through carefully. The first tent he came to was empty, large enough to house about ten people. There were this number of wooden-army cots lying empty, some folded up in a pile in the middle of the floor. He let the canvas door drop to behind him.

As he turned away he realised he was being watched. Across the clearing stood a man, completely immobile. In his arms he held what looked like a pile of clothes. Tanner waved and called a greeting but the man made no move to reply. He seemed apprehensive. He must have heard the plane coming in – had no one been told they were arriving? Tanner walked quickly to one of the Portakabins, which seemed to be constructed from old packing cases and bits of sheet plastic tacked into place. He climbed the two steps to the doorway and peered inside.

It was a long dark room, with several benches laid out with mechanical instruments. At first he thought it was deserted, then he heard a sound from the far corner. Taking a couple of steps to the far side he looked down the aisle. At the bottom of the room a man crouched forward over the desk. There was a small desk lamp hanging over his head, and the sound of classical music coming from a tape player by his elbow.

'Hello?'

There was no reply. Tanner walked down the room. The man, who was about thirty-eight or so, was hunched forward cutting slide sections, his hands covered in mud. He looked up as Tanner approached. 'Who are you?'

'Are you the only one here?' asked Tanner.

'They're all away,' said the small wiry man, who sounded American. He looked Tanner over carefully. 'Are you lost?'

'No,' said Tanner. 'We've just flown down from Khartoum to . . .' he paused. 'Visit.'

'Oh,' nodded the man. 'I see.' They stared at each other for a moment, then he went back to his work. He looked up again a moment later and seemed surprised to see Tanner still standing there. He put down the drill again. 'Are you staying long?'

'Just a few days, I think,' said Tanner.

'Well, there's a big tent out there on the far side. It'll be empty

101

for the next few days while they're away, you can use that.' He indicated the direction with a spatula he was holding. Tanner was about to say thank you when there was a sound from behind him. He turned to see Gilmour in the doorway.

'Tanner?' he called out uncertainly.

'Over here.'

There was a moment while Gilmour found his way through the benches, Spooner the pilot right behind him. They were looking round them as they came over.

'We were wondering what had happened to you,' said Gilmour.

'How many of you are there?' asked the scientist.

Gilmour stepped forward, hand out to grip his muddy fingers. 'Gilmour, Charlie Gilmour. There are two of us, myself and Tanner. This is Mr Spooner, our pilot. He will be going back tonight.'

Spooner shook his head. 'No, I don't think so, mate – too dark now.'

Gilmour nodded and then turned back to the small man. 'And you are . . . ?'

'Whitman,' he said, pushing the round spectacles back on to his nose. 'Stan Whitman, but as I told your friend here,' he indicated Tanner with the spatula, flicking mud about, 'I'm the only one here at the moment.'

'Where is everyone else?' asked Gilmour, looking round the room as though expecting to see the rest of them appear from behind the lab benches.

'They're all away, all about in the field on a big seismic thing.'

'Well,' said Gilmour, raising his eyebrows, 'I was told that you would be expecting me. I've just flown in from the States especially.'

'To see this place?' Whitman sounded incredulous.

Gilmour leaned back on the bench and cross his arms. 'Perhaps you could give me an idea, Mr Whitman, on the operation in its present state.'

Whitman looked round the assembled visitors carefully, scratching at the surface of the bench with his spatula. Out through the chicken-wire windows, Tanner could see a small fire was being started. The washing man and another stood round fanning the flames. Whitman stood up and went over to light the hurricane lamp. He came back to sit down before speaking.

'What we have here is a dead duck.' He waved a hand to indicate the cluttered desk where he was working. 'There's nothing here but oil shale. Oil shale and a bit of tar in places. Apart from that, no petroleum.'

Tanner glanced across at Gilmour who was nodding slowly to all this. He had not expected to be briefed so frankly. Gilmour was reaching for a menthol cigarette and his lighter. He exhaled a long stream of smoke into the air.

'You don't sound very hopeful. I was led to believe that the picture was a little more optimistic.'

'Mr Gilmour, I've been sitting in this dump for six months now and I haven't seen anything to indicate different. Mind you, it's a huge damn country; it could be anywhere.'

Gilmour smiled. 'For a scientist you seem to have a very fatalistic view of things.'

Whitman shrugged. 'Take it any way you want.' He went back to shuffling bits of paper and rock around the desk with his muddied hands. He pushed the spectacles back up his nose and took the cigarette which Tanner offered. He leaned forward for a light.

'I remember you now,' he said. 'I met you once at a party.'

Tanner nodded, smiling as he remembered where he had seen Whitman before. It had been a birthday party for someone, and Whitman had started a fight with a nasty-looking marine from the American embassy. Though a small man, he had a fierce temper. He scratched his head now, the wispy hair scattered round the widening bald patch.

'Is there somewhere we can put our things?' asked Gilmour. Whitman repeated the information about the tent they could use and Gilmour left the room. Spooner wanted to get back to his plane to lock it up for the night. Tanner followed Whitman out of the room.

'He seems like cheerful company, your friend,' Whitman said, holding the lamp up to light up the steps.

'He's come a long way for this,' said Tanner.

'Haven't we all,' answered Whitman glibly. They walked across the compound towards the area around the tree which served as the kitchen. The two men sitting by the fire looked up as they approached.

'Hey, Benny, is there nothing to eat tonight or what?' called Whitman.

Benjamin and Abraham were the two cooks. Benjamin laughed and stood up. Pulling a torn shirt over his head, he walked over to the mess tent.

The whole camp seemed to be waiting for something – the return of the field party, perhaps. The station had been gradually stripped down over the last few months; staff pulled out, resources cancelled. The reasons were varied: a lack of success, the escalating hostilities. The armies of the South were increasing their actions partly because of the rumours that oil was about to be discovered right on their doorstep. If the wealth was uncovered, they said, then the benefits would be kept safely in the North by the government. The field station was being drawn slowly into the conflict.

A meal was duly produced and they all ate together. Afterwards Whitman retired to his tent and Spooner said he had to get an early start. He was sleeping in the same tent as Tanner and Gilmour, who found themselves sitting alone.

'He seems a little down about the whole thing,' said Tanner, referring to Whitman.

'It is no more than I expected,' said Gilmour. 'This place is a shambles. There is oil here – I have seen the evidence myself. There's oil here all right,' he repeated, gazing round the deserted camp. 'It's just a question of resources and application.'

Tanner nodded his head. He was unclear in what capacity he was expected to act. As far as Thompson was concerned they had asked for someone who had some local ability, but he thought that it would be easier to get along with Gilmour if in general he concurred with the American's line of thought. He was content just to be out here. He realised now that he had needed to get away; he needed a change of scenery. There was a sense of freedom out here in the open. It was a relief to be away from the hollow walls of the city.

When he got back to town Nina would be gone. It was as simple as that. They had never really said goodbye. He didn't want to think about the fact that she was probably out of his life for ever. He had decided on the flight this morning that when he went back, it would be for the last time. He was going to leave the country for good. He had given it three, nearly four years now and it was clear that what he had hoped to find here had eluded him again and again. It was pointless to stay on any longer. It seemed he would always be a tourist here, a foreigner anyway. It was time to try somewhere else. If he was a foreigner both here and in Britain, then he would be a foreigner wherever he went and therefore he could go anywhere. The idea of going back to the low ceilings and the narrow smoke-stained walls of England didn't much appeal. Home was nowhere in particular, so anywhere would do. He just had to get up and go.

As he walked over to the tent, Tanner remembered being told once that this place had been part of a slave trade route in the last century. This was a stopping-off point, a meeting place for marauding gangs who consolidated their catches, slaves for the Arabs in the north. Through the swamplands and the open ground they dragged their net, gradually building up their herds of human subordination. On a grand scale they had learned to evade the river boat patrols and bribe the officials. It was a lucrative business. Women and children were dragged kicking and screaming into a life of servitude, chained up and haltered by the neck, feet hobbled and barely fed. If you listened carefully you could hear the cry of the children in the creak of the big old trees that stood sentinel round the sleeping camp.

The engine of the Land Rover woke Tanner up in the early hours. It was still dark – the hands of his watch said it was just after half-past two. He climbed out of his army cot and pulled on his trousers. Stepping out into the night, he was caught in the glare of the headlights and held up a hand to shield his eyes. He stepped aside.

'Stan, is that you?' came a voice.

'No, it's me, Tanner.' There was no reply. 'I'm one of the group that flew down today.'

Tanner moved round until he could see the man who had just climbed out of the Land Rover. He was of average build, maybe slightly overweight, in his early thirties. He looked up at Tanner.

'Hello, Tanner, I'm Hays, station manager.' He was busy collecting a bag and some maps from the seat. 'You got here all right then?'

Tanner nodded. 'Are you alone?' he asked.

'There's hardly anyone left out here. I left the team there to run some core tests and a seismic probe.' He paused, looking at Tanner. 'But I mean there's only three of them.' He picked up the rest of his things and kicked the car door shut behind him. 'I came back to meet this man.' He stopped. 'What's his name again?'

'Gilmour,' said Tanner.

'Well, I was too late to catch him anyway, I'll see him tomorrow.' Tanner nodded in agreement. 'Well, he's met Whitman already,' he said carefully.

Hays winced. 'So he knows how bad things are then?'

Tanner shrugged. 'I don't think he was really expecting this.'

Hays looked at Tanner for a moment. 'You're his escort, are you?'

Tanner smiled. 'Yes, I suppose so.'

Hays paused and looked carefully at Tanner again. 'Where did you get that accent?' he asked, smiling.

Tanner's back stiffened. 'Sheffield. I used to live there.'

'Ah,' nodded Hayes. 'Thought I recognised it, I'm a Geordie meself. Studying over there, were you?'

'No, I lived there.' Tanner found himself hesitating. 'I was born there.' It never sounded right somehow.

'Oh I see,' said Hays, smiling again. He readjusted the things under his arm and started towards his tent. He stopped once more.

'How long will you be staying?'

'I don't know,' said Tanner. 'It really depends on Mr Gilmour. Soon as he's seen what he came for, I suppose.'

Hays nodded, then he scratched his chest through his open shirt. 'He's not American, is he? he asked cautiously. Tanner nodded in reply.

'Well,' sighed Hays, 'maybe it'll help them make their minds up about what they're going to do about this mess.' He paused before going on. 'The government don't want us here, because of the danger. The rebels don't want us here because as far as they're concerned we represent the government, and if we find anything a lot of people are going to be better off and the rebels won't be among them. The company is praying that we find something and quickly, but they have to hedge their bets. So they cut us down to a minimum and that way if anything does happen to us they lose as little as possible.' He shrugged and held his hands out.

'Is there a chance then that Gilmour is right? I mean, do you think there is something down here?' asked Tanner.

Hays took a step towards Tanner. The lights from the Land Rover had been left on. 'I wouldn't still be down here if I didn't think it was worth looking. If I was absolutely certain there was nothing here at all then I'd be away. If we can get the oil and get out before the rebels shut us down, then we'll have our claim. I mean, we're not the only people out here – the place is crawling with survey teams; all the big boys are here. If we can just make a claim, then we can pull out and let the two sides fight it out.'

'Have you had any trouble with the fighting?'

'Trouble? I don't know, it's not that we're in any immediate danger. They come out from time to time and kidnap someone. Usually a nurse or something, or someone from one of the big companies, I mean I have my doubts about whether our lot could afford the ransom if one of us got taken.' He laughed at his own joke, adding, 'I mean, if they wanted to shut us down, they could I suppose do it quite easily. Perhaps.'

'Perhaps they know we're not going to find anything here,' suggested Tanner.

Hays smiled at the effort. 'Well, I wish they'd let us in on it.' He paused and looked round the camp. 'I think what worries me more

107

is the possibility of an accident. You don't get a second chance with those rockets, and it seems they're hitting any plane they see.' There was a moment of silence.

'How long will he be staying, do you think?' he asked for the second time.

'A week at the most, I would think.'

'You think he would really want to stay down here for a whole week?' smiled Hays.

There was no way of knowing what Gilmour wanted to do. He seemed pretty much set on finding out what he had come here for; until that was achieved there would be no going back. Hays was tired. He picked up his bag again from the ground and saying goodnight he turned and disappeared into his tent, calling to Tanner from the entrance to turn off the lights of the Land Rover.

Tanner wandered back to the vehicle and reached inside for the switch. The camp fell into the darkness that clung to the edge of the clearing.

Tanner was woken again in the early morning, by the pilot, who needed someone to help with the plane.

They walked back across the field to the landing strip. It was just about dawn, the air cool and refreshing from the night before. Smoke was gently rising from the wood fire Benjamin was stoking up. He muttered a greeting. Everyone was speaking in muted tones, as though wary of breaking the spell of the night that still lingered there in the quiet air. As Tanner and Spooner neared the landing strip the birds were waking up and the trees were full of chattering life.

The turned the plane round and Tanner stood to one side while Spooner carried out his checks. Everything was okay. Spooner slapped on his sunglasses and waved through the small window.

'See you soon,' shouted Tanner over the roar of the engines. He stood back as the plane rolled away, and then strolled back to the camp, which was gradually coming to life. Benjamin's fire was burning slowly under the shelter of the large tree by the mess tent. He and Abraham were speaking in low voices, pausing as Tanner joined them by the fire. He sat down on the edge of the bed, a rope-strung cradle trailing strands to the ground. A glass of milky tea was passed to him and the conversation resumed. Rubbing his eyes, Tanner peered through the grey light that hung over the dusty canvas of his tent. The other cot was empty; there was no sign of Gilmour.

Tanner asked Benjamin, 'The *americani* Gilmour – do you know where he is?'

'He went away while you were at the aeroplane.'

So Gilmour had got up while Tanner was helping Spooner and wandered off by himself somewhere.

The sun was creeping slowly up through the sparse covering of trees with their chirping birds. Whitman appeared now across the clearing, scratching armpits and buckling trouser belt. He yawned, stretching out his arms, and sat down on a folding deckchair by the fire where eggs were now being fried. Fresh eggs from the chickens kicking and squabbling in a small pen behind the cook area.

'How long have you been out here then?' asked Tanner.

Whitman squinted myopically, finished polishing his spectacles and put them back on. 'Months, absolutely months, I can't remember how long. Mind you, it's a lot better now that Gary's here. The feller that was here before was a pain in the ass. He didn't know anything.'

Tanner wondered what kind of family this man had and where they were. He asked when he had been home last.

'I left East St Louis about fifteen years ago. I haven't been back since – I got no reason to, really. I have a sister in San Diego but I don't know where.' The egg clung to the hairs of his blond moustache.

'What do I want to go back for? I got all I need here . . . well, perhaps some things could be a little more available, like women for example.'

There were two small children sitting in the open doorway of the hut that was behind the cooking area where the chickens clucked and stuttered. The hut was where Benjamin and his family lived. Abraham, the younger of the two brothers, slept outside on a bed

109

in front of the hut, which had been built of packing cases and plastic sheeting. The two small children sat and watched the world from the doorway. The extended family outnumbered the rest of the camp in its present form. The final member was a baby of about six months who travelled everywhere cradled in his mother's arms.

'Fancy a look around today? May as well take advantage of the truck being here.' Tanner agreed to go along with Whitman, who had a round of various survey points to investigate.

Hays joined them at breakfast, picking up a glass of tea and reaching for the plate of eggs passed to him. He began to discuss with Whitman the state of affairs of the team he had left behind. They had decided to run a core test on an area about twenty miles away. The drill team consisted of two general hands and two technicians. They had enough food for a week. The roads they had to use were little more than tracks cut through by an advance vehicle.

There was still no sign of Gilmour about half an hour later when Tanner joined Whitman by the Land Rover. The American was pumping petrol from a barrel into a jerrycan.

'This could well be the only damn gas you or I are ever going to find round here,' he said wryly.

Tanner laughed and helped carry over the next can. They loaded up the Land Rover and then Whitman had to go and consult with Hays to decide exactly where they would be going.

Tanner sat in the passenger seat, his eyes closed, until Benjamin knocked on the door of the Land Rover. Tanner opened his eyes and the man handed him a canvas water bag, which could be slung out of the window where the breeze would cool it as they drove along.

'Thanks,' said Tanner, taking the bag. Benjamin started to walk away, then Tanner called him back, asking, 'Any sign of Gilmour yet?'

Benjamin shook his head, and headed back to the mess tent. Tanner sat for a moment then jumped down, deciding to look for Gilmour. Whitman was just coming back.

'Ready to go?' asked Tanner.

'Sure, let's get out there before it really gets hot.' Whitman jumped into the driving seat and pulled the door to.

'What's up?' he asked, seeing Tanner hesitating before getting back in.

'I just wanted to check on Gilmour.'

'Oh, don't worry about him,' dismissed Whitman, revving the engine into life.

'So where have you come from then?'

Tanner baulked at the question, saying nothing for the moment as the Land Rover jumped across a hump in the road. The noise of the engine made it difficult to hear; they had to shout to make themselves heard. He described in as few words as possible the circumstances that had led him to this place. He couldn't tell if Whitman could hear him or not. In his turn the American rambled on, not discouraged by the noise, until they pulled up beside a small outcrop. Tanner carried the bag and Whitman took the readings.

'You see,' continued Whitman, warming to his theme, 'out here everything is so simple. You wake up in the morning, under an open sky I might add, and you work and you eat and then you sleep again.' He held his hands out. 'I mean, what more could you ask for that wouldn't complicate things? Women? I tried that marriage thing and it never worked. She thinks I'm dead, has no idea where I am.' He stopped for a second. 'If she did she'd probably sue me for all I've got.' He laughed as they began to unpack his charts again. 'Fact is I've got the whole thing covered. When I die she gets forty thousand dollars on my life insurance – that's just in case, you know.' He pointed at the sky then he lowered his finger a fraction. 'Do you believe in God and all that stuff?'

'I don't know, really.'

'Well, it's a tough one, but the way I see it, you can never be too sure.'

They finished at the first location and drove on to the second one, a small dried-up lake bed. Whitman talked non-stop for most of the time. Tanner carried on listening. He found Whitman an

111

interesting person, but more than this there was nothing to detract from the fact that for the moment there was no need to look for any reason. There was a job that had to be done and they went about it, and that was it.

'So what will you do when you go back with him?'

They had stopped for a rest and something to eat. Whitman chewed on a piece of cheese. Tanner didn't need to think about the answer; he had already made up his mind.

'I'm going away.'

'Leaving the country? Where will you go, back to Britain?'

Tanner shook his head. He wasn't completely sure about the next bit. 'Somewhere different, perhaps the Far East.'

'Ah, the Far East,' said Whitman in mock English. 'I've done all that trip – India, Japan, all that stuff, Bangkok.'

Tanner laughed. 'Is there anything you haven't done?'

'I'm only kidding. Don't matter where you've been, what matters is what you've seen there.' He paused for a moment. 'Who said that?'

Tanner replied, 'I don't think I know. Probably you just made it up.'

'Probably I did.' Whitman reached into his bag and produced a small flat tin. Inside the tin were a number of rolled-up cigarettes. Selecting one, Whitman rotated it gently between his fingers before lighting it. He took a few puffs and offered the joint to Tanner.

'That's it, man, we'll call it a day,' said Whitman, placing a foot on the dashboard.

In the late afternoon the whole world seemed silent; nothing seemed to stir. They sat and talked about what Whitman regarded as much his country as anybody else's. They smoked another of his roll-ups.

'This war will never come to an end until someone, one individual, emerges who is strong enough to hold the whole thing together as one country.

'Just one man with the strength and the vision to hold everyone's attention. But he'll have to be a crazy bastard because he'll more than likely have to die for what he believes,' continued Whitman.

'Some say that Meru is that man,' said Tanner.

'Who can say? Some say that he's the man, and some say he's just another crazy bastard.'

'But supposing he was the one?'

'I suppose only time will tell. You just have to look around to see that things take a long time to happen in a place like this.' Whitman reached forward for the ignition. Tanner reached out to stop him. 'Wait.' He pointed out through the windscreen. In a thin clump of trees straight ahead of them, a small antelope was nosing out of the cover head down.

'Now that's got to be worth coming down here for. Makes a change from all them vultures hanging round that spider web of a capital you live in, eh?'

Tanner nodded at the comparison. The antelope paused, looking up suddenly.

'Uh-oh, must have smelled the reefer. Don't move,' said Whitman.

The antelope watched them for a moment, then went back to what it was doing.

'What is it doing?' asked Tanner.

'She's looking for food, nosing about something that she's found there.'

'She's not eating though – not chewing, I mean, is she?'

The antelope stepped carefully and looking back once she moved away into the trees. Whitman had a pair of field glasses which he peered through.

'One of her sisters or brothers – bones of another deer, a dead relative.' He passed the glasses to Tanner who could see the small pointed skull and the hollow sockets which stared back at him.

Whitman started the van and they drove back to the camp in the falling evening.

Gilmour was waiting in the empty lab room.

'Where've you been?'

113

Tanner did not detect the edge in the man's voice. He could hear Whitman moving around in the room behind him.

'Out with Stan here. I was just giving him a hand with things.'

The explanation met a moment's silence and Tanner looked up from the samples he was putting away.

'What's up? Did I do something wrong?'

'You're here to help me, not Whitman. They've been working out here for several months now. I think they can manage the workload by themselves.'

Tanner began to smile, then he straightened his face.

'I work for this company. This is the kind of work I do.'

'I wanted to take a look around some of the sights myself.'

The situation seemed almost absurd to Tanner. He found himself wondering if Whitman could hear the conversation.

'There was nothing to stop you coming with us.'

'No, no of course not.' A change came over Gilmour; he seemed to sense the absurdity himself. He stood up and moved to leave the room. He stopped as he passed Tanner.

'I'm sorry for sounding so abrupt. Its just that I like to know what's going on.' He managed a half smile.

'Sure,' replied Tanner.' I understand. It's a bit difficult out here.'

Gilmour nodded and said no more. After he had left the room Tanner sat down for a moment and thought it over. Perhaps things between them were getting a little more strained.

In his dream Tanner was exhausted. He was aware of having walked for thousands of miles, mile upon mile of empty landscape that surrounded him. There was someone else – he wasn't alone. There was someone behind him, someone following him. He had the sense that the person had been with him all the way. There was a common aim which they had ahead of them, a place. Somewhere ahead of them was a place where they would be safe. The sun came across the sky alongside him. There was nowhere he could turn to, there was not a scrap of shelter in sight. The sand that covered his feet was alive, slipping and shifting like the back of a great awesome beast over which he now crept cautiously, careful not to wake it from its uneasy slumber. He could feel the unsteady breathing through the soles of his bare feet which burned in the sand.

Now a train like a long dark snake drew a line across the horizon between the sky and the land. Silent but alive, the train gave out a plume of grey smoke that sketched lines on the painted ceiling of the ultramarine sky. The smoke from the train seemed to bend and grow, flowing, into the sky like a dye that infiltrated everything it touched. Dark rain-heavy clouds appeared in the smoke and formed into a mosaic of oppressive weight. A roll of thunder reeled around his head and the lightning crackled in his hair. He threw back his head and howled at the brewing storm. He was asking a question and there was a reply though he could not make out the words.

Turning round, he realised that he was not alone. The old man who had been following him for days was there, a few yards away. He was wearing what seemed to be a pair of shorts. In his hand he carried a smooth staff with which he tapped the ground by his feet. The old man seemed to be saying that what was about to happen was of no importance. In his dream Tanner knew that what he had to say was of vital importance, but what was it? What was it that he had to say?

The wind hummed in anticipation, the lightning flickered expectantly and the thunder rumbled. But the train had rolled off across the horizon and was lost in the whirling cloud.

For Tanner the next few days passed easily. Long slow mornings, waking with the change in the light. Sitting in the shade of the big tree watching the children chase each other around. Benjamin and Abraham would go off to collect wood and dung for the fires. Benjamin's wife would watch over the children from the doorway and often helped with carrying wood, balancing it on her head in a bundle. On occasion Tanner would help Whitman in the lab. He seemed to be always busy on one thing or another. Whitman was after all a scientist, and his attention to detail was an addiction. He

115

would describe what he was doing in minute definition, often going on long after he'd left Tanner behind. Surrounded by microscopes and drills and chemical tubes, he was completely immersed in his own findings. The rest of the world which he was dissecting so carefully came to a halt when it reached the doorway.

Gilmour spent his days reading up on the work done here. He borrowed a section of what was really Hays's office, a compartment in the second Portakabin. Hays gave him access to all the field reports that had been written since the the field station had started up nearly two years ago. Hays also gave him his own journal and the station manager's log which had been started by the previous manager, Heron. Tanner saw little of Gilmour, who seemed to be preoccupied to a degree that was almost obsession. Hays and Whitman noticed it also, though little was said directly.

'What is he here for exactly? I mean, is it to balance the books or what?' asked Whitman one evening when the three of them had eaten by themselves, Gilmour remaining at work in the office.

'He's here to check that everything is being done to achieve our objective,' said Hays carefully.

'Which it isn't,' finished Whitman.

'Which it isn't,' agreed Hays, 'not through any fault of ours, though.'

Hays was slightly drunk now – they all were. Whitman had produced a bottle of *aaraqui* from somewhere and the raw spirit was buzzing through Tanner's head. Since arriving here he had been having a series of dreams. Almost every night, in fact. The dreams were similar each time: a place, open, desolate, a sense of despair which conflicted with the fact that here he felt more relaxed and comfortable than he could remember in months.

The conversation turned back to work, and the field team that was working on the core drilling. They had had five days to get started and Hays wanted to get back and find out how they were getting on.

'I think Mr Gilmour will want to come along – in fact he has told me he intends to,' said Hays.

'You mean I have to stay here on my own?' asked Whitman.

116

Hays shrugged. 'You mean you don't want to stay here on your own?'

'This place is haunted, you know, haunted by the ghosts of all those shackled souls that were bled to death in this very spot.' Whitman leaned forwards in his chair. The fire flickered in his spectacles, casting crimson light round the faces assembled. The flames threw hazy shadows leaping through the diesel blackness around them. Hays began to laugh. 'Don't start that again.'

But Whitman was pausing only to draw another breath. 'Small boys with frail legs and young girls with sarcophagus eyes; buried alive by slavery.' He stopped and took another drink from his glass.

'Why don't you come with us, then, Stan? said Hays finally.

'Good of you to ask, Gary,' nodded Whitman.

Gilmour was coming across the camp now. Under one arm he carried his large notebook which he seemed to have with him all the time.

'Good evening, gentlemen.' He spoke without sitting down, not intending to stay long. Hays leaned forwards in his chair as though about to stand.

'Did you get any further with it?'

Gilmour nodded distractedly. 'There's still plenty to do. I understand that you will be on your way out to the drill rig in the next couple of days. If that's the case then I think it's important that I come along with you.'

'Sure,' nodded Hays. 'That's no problem. I think in all probability it'll be Friday afternoon. You'd be welcome to come along,' he smiled. Gilmour returned the smile and then made his excuse and said goodnight.

'For a black man he sure is tight-assed,' muttered Whitman.

'You shouldn't let yourself be subject to these racial stereotypes,' said Hays. Whitman looked at him to see if he was winding him up, which he was. He poured everyone another drink, then he addressed Tanner.

'You've see more of him than any of us. What do you think?'

'I think he's just trying to do his job, that's all,' said Tanner.

117

'That's all right, but what do you really think about him? You can tell us, we're all friends here,' glinted Whitman.

Tanner lit another cigarette and thought about how long these two had been out here living this strange solitary existence. Gilmour must have been the oddest kind of visitor they might have expected. Whitman was hiding away from the world and its cares, burying himself in the dials and readings of science, living secure in the knowledge that no one would come this far off the beaten track to locate him. He had told Tanner that he had spent countless years in one part of the remote world after another. There was a sense in which both men saw Gilmour as a threat. For Whitman it was a reminder of the order of the world outside, while Hays perhaps for different reasons knew that the outcome of Gilmour's investigations could affect his career. For Hays this posting was an opportunity that could either make or break his future as a station manager. Unlike Whitman, Hays was a father and a husband. His family lived in Britain, a small village in the North East outside Stockton. Taking the job was a risk, both to his family life and to his career. If they were successful then he would emerge in good favour. There were few enough people with stable jobs in this industry. The alternative was not attractive – home to the dole queue even. So for Hays the easy-going attitude which Whitman generated was no more than a diversion; he didn't live the life, he just subscribed from time to time.

'Uranium,' announced Whitman, bringing Tanner back from his thoughts.

'Uranium?' repeated Tanner.

Whitman wiped his mouth with the back of his hand and pushed his spectacles back up his nose. 'Uranium, that's where the money is. You can sell it for a fortune.' He paused to belch. 'I know for a fact that there is a world trade market going on in this very country.' His voice slowed to emphasise every word. 'Right under our very noses.'

Hays shook his head in disbelief. Whitman waved his hand in Tanner's face. 'No, its true. All I have to do, the way I figure it, is find where I can get the damn stuff from. I know it's all out there. This country is loaded when it comes to uranium.'

'So where are you going to start looking then?' asked Tanner.

Whitman shrugged. 'Who knows? I mean, I don't even have a geiger counter.' He erupted into a fit of giggles.

Tanner and Hays carried the American back to his cot and settled him in carefully.

'You think he'll be all right?' asked Tanner.

'I'm sure he's had years of practice at this kind of thing,' replied Hays.

They left him and went back to their own cots.

The desert alive now in the deep west with the scurry of feet fleeing the dry breath of wind that failed once again to bring any glimpse of hope. The life that these people lived depended on a thin line between nature and man which offered an existence: that line had now closed up and they were left at the mercy of the landscape which was their home. The bitter feuding between rival factions or families or tribes was not lost in this struggle for life. If it was then it would of course only be in those individual instances of people meeting. On the larger scale the raids still continued as they had always done, thieving and killing in some cases. The people were armed now with modern automatic weapons, the hostility metamorphosed.

In the light of all this the government did little to alleviate the situation. There was little that could be done, they said. The fighting went on hardly hindered by the efforts of the inadequately trained and armed police force. The massacres took place; the burning train filled with refugees fleeing from nothing more or less than unhindered hatred. The dying lifestyle of the Kabbabish, who now found that the government's suggestions that they expand their herds was coming back on them as the wells dried up.

Everywhere the exodus from the hounding skeleton plea of drought went on as it must do. They came across the border from Chad, fleeing their own war. There are no borders in the face of adversity and besides there was little or nothing that the troops could do to patrol the hundreds of miles of open land. The war in the neighbouring country was only a coincidence of geography; to the south the same thing was happening as the Eritreans took to the road ahead of the army: there own army.

The block line of the train drew a trail of smoke across the gaping horizon.

THIRTEEN

The burnt-out derrick lay twisted and dying in the scorched earth. Black acrid smoke from the tyres smouldered, stinging the men's eyes. There was a flicker of flame around the upturned cabin, lingering as if to make sure its job was complete. The derrick lay stretched out across the clearing. The Land Rover lay on its side and the remaining poles which supported the cabin were all that was left of it. There was no sign of any of the team that had been working here. The smell of petrol filled the air.

'How the fuck did this happen then?' said Hays, looking round at the mess. Whitman was shaking his head. 'Some kind of explosion caused the fire, I think.'

'Petrol explosion or something, could it be?'

'They had a good store of petrol here, there was a lot of it here,' said Whitman.

The four of them, Whitman, Hays, Gilmour and Tanner, stood around in the aftermath looking for a clue.

'I don't think . . .' Whitman faltered, looking into the upturned vehicle. 'I don't think there's anyone in there.'

'There would be some kind of remains, I suppose,' said Tanner.

'I suppose so,' said Hays. 'How much though, I wouldn't know.'

'Bones,' said Gilmour. 'If there was any kind of explosion then fragments of bone would have been flung far enough not to have been totally consumed.'

'You mean they might not be here then?' asked Hays, who seemed somewhat relieved by the possibility. Gilmour shrugged his shoulders.

'It's hard to say at this stage.'

It was late afternoon and the light was starting to fade. They decided to move away a bit from the wreck for the night.

'There's not much else we can do now,' said Whitman to himself, stepping back.

The sun set on the wreck and the three men retired, leaving Gilmour to wander round in the shadows looking for any kind of evidence for whatever he thought had happened.

If there had been any method by which Tanner could have predicted what was to confront them here then he would have avoided the confrontation. He had enjoyed the few days of peace and quiet down here. He had liked the feeling of living back in the land; the country for the city. Things were clearer out here. Faced with the sight of the charred remains of rig and possibly men, he had the sense that this was predictable in some way, that something as violent was bound to have happened, if only to remind him that things were not to be taken for granted. That Gilmour's presence was not without its darker side. At the same time he felt like shouting out, protesting at the top of his voice against this seemingly inevitable cycle of death: the vicious cut of night through the middle of day.

They sat together, Whitman, Tanner and Hays, all around the small fire. They were a few hundred yards from the wreck and there was a lingering smell from the smoke that seemed to have infected the earth. They were each locked away, it seemed, in their own thoughts. Whitman tried to cheer up the proceedings by producing a bottle which they passed around.

'Do you think they all died in that?' asked Whitman, jerking his thumb unnecessarily in the direction of the wreck.

'Why would anyone want to kill them?' He was asking himself questions, it appeared. At least no one else was making an attempt to answer him.

'Its called war, Stan, that's what they do in wars, they kill each other,' said Hays at last.

'They weren't in the war,' pointed out Whitman. 'They had nothing to do with it.'

'Don't get sentimental about it, Stan. This is what happens. People get hurt in the middle of these things.' Hays tried to convince Whitman, looking to Tanner for support, who confirmed,

'He's right. I'm sure it's not that odd. It's just a shock when you're so close to it.'

'It's just like everything else, then, is that it?' enquired Whitman. 'It never happens to you, always someone else.'

'Stan, you're not telling me that you'd rather have been burned to death in there instead of one of those boys, are you?' asked Hays, whose voice seemed laced with just a touch of irritation.

''Course not,' grumbled Whitman. 'But what I'd like to know is, what is he doing, exactly?'

The other two looked over Whitman's shoulder to where Gilmour was wandering round the site of the wreck with a torch. They could see the light from his hand brush over the ground back and forth.

'I really don't know and I don't care,' announced Hays. 'I'm getting some sleep.' He rolled into his sleeping bag and the others eventually did the same.

By morning nothing much had changed. Tanner woke to find the others still asleep. He felt dusty and in need of a wash. He stood up and shook his boots before pulling them on. The sun was just breaking over the horizon and the sky was a shade of azure. The clearing they were in was littered with bags and bits of clothing. The empty bottle lay on its side.

He walked back round the camp and ended up next to the wreck. He touched the burnt twisted metal and the jagged edges of the machine. He stepped across a wheel hub and two birds leapt chirping to the air.

'One of them got away.'

Tanner turned to find Gilmour standing behind him.

'What?'

'It looks like they killed two of them but there was another – probably away from the main area – who managed to escape,' said Gilmour. He sounded to Tanner as if he had rehearsed the lines. A bad actor, surmised Tanner. It simply added to his apprehension. He didn't trust Gilmour and the more he heard from him the less likely it was that he ever would.

122

'So one got away,' said Tanner slowly. 'You can tell that from the tracks?'

Gilmour smiled. 'I'm not a Red Indian, Tanner, but someone was coming back with a reel of steel wire when the attack happened. He dropped it and ran. It's lying over there.' He pointed. Tanner was thinking that he really understood nothing about Gilmour. If you believe that the facts of one's life determine the lines of the face then Gilmour's face was a puzzle. If it was true that anything could be read from the wrinkles and the scars to the shape of his eyes and the curl of his mouth, then this face said nothing to Tanner. All these features had been rendered anonymous in Gilmour's case. The lines had a dull shade of transience. Gilmour was invisible.

'You understand what I mean, then?' asked Gilmour.

Tanner nodded his head though he couldn't say he knew why. He sat down on an upturned jerrycan.

'There's nothing more that we can do here, then?'

'Not for the moment,' answered Gilmour.

Hays and Whitman emerged from the bush.

'You sure you should be smoking round here so soon?'

'There's nothing left to burn, it's all gone.'

They all stood around in the clearing. There was nothing more for them to do, there was very little that could be salvaged. Hays wanted to know if all the drill heads had been located.

Whitman was wandering listlessly through the wreckage. 'I hope those guys are all right.'

'You think they'll still be alive?'

'I don't know. What do you think, Charlie?'

'I haven't seen enough to form a conclusion yet,' said Gilmour.

Whitman smiled to himself.

Hays was in a hurry now to return. They climbed back into the Land Rover and started the long journey back.

The following day passed slowly. Hays was concerned that an effort was made to pack up and get out. The next service plane was

123

due the day after and he and Whitman were both determined to be on it, or at least ready to go if need be. Gilmour spent the day poring over maps and charts in his tent. He emerged around midday to join the others for lunch. They all sat round the table under the tree while Benjamin and Abraham served out a hot meal.

'I can't believe it's time to leave,' said Whitman, mouth full.

'We have no choice at this stage. I mean, it would be stupid to stay.' Hays paused to look round the group before continuing. 'I mean, we are all agreed that it was no accident?'

'I am certain it was no accident,' said Gilmour softly.

'Well, personally I'm satisfied that it wasn't, so I think as leader of . . .'

Whitman interrupted. 'Cut the crap, Gary. We're going back, okay?'

'I just want it to be clear.'

'There's no point,' said Tanner, 'in waiting to find out what happens next.'

'It's the only decision to take, Gary. They'll understand when we get back. I mean, this is a goddamn war zone here.' Whitman tapped the table furiously.

Gilmour cleared his throat and leaned forward in his chair, the canvas creaking in the silence.

'Well, gentlemen, I believe that in your position I would probably come to the same conclusion. So I hope that you can appreciate that my stance is slightly different due to my position.'

'What are you trying to say?' asked Tanner.

Gilmour turned to look directly at Tanner. 'It's simple. I don't feel at this stage that my job here is complete.'

'You mean you want to stay on?' asked Hays.

'Yes, I intend to do so,' answered Gilmour evenly.

Tanner had perhaps been expecting something like this. The way that the American had been preoccupied with the details of the wreck ever since they'd found it – it was almost as though this were what he had made the journey for. But more interestingly Tanner felt that there was a note of uncertainty in his voice, as though he were almost going through the motions.

'You're sure this is what you want to do?'

'I know what I'm doing, believe me,' answered Gilmour. Tanner was convinced that this was the worst idea he had ever come across. The American wanted to drive back in the direction of the burned-out rig and start looking for more clues – clues to what, he didn't elaborate on. Tanner's obligation to look after the man was just about reaching its limits.

'You don't have to come along if you don't want to.'

'I'm curious,' said Tanner, sitting down on his cot. They were back in the tent they shared, Gilmour studying the maps he kept in a small case. He put down his pencil.

'I mean, are you some sort of spy, an agent for the government or what?'

'I'm an observer. I am actually an employee of the same company that pays your wages, as you know. I've been asked to just have a careful look round.'

'Sounds like spying to me,' said Tanner. 'Why did they pick you?'

Gilmour paused and lit one of his cigarettes. 'They picked me because of previous experience which I have in this field.'

'You mean you used to be a spy, is that it?'

Gilmour shrugged. 'Just think of me as an observer.'

'So just how close are you intending to observe?' asked Tanner, continuing on his tack.

'I just want to take a look around, see what the level of activity is.' Gilmour shrugged again and held out a hand palm up. 'I'm doing no more than a journalist investigating a story would do. That doesn't make me a spy, does it?'

'If that's the case why don't we all go home and read the paper?'

Gilmour stubbed out his cigarette and leaned forward in the chair. 'When I asked for somebody with good ground knowledge I expected someone with just a little enthusiasm. Perhaps I was a shade optimistic. But I think that it's not too much to ask that you at least carry out the job as best you can. That is what you are being paid for, after all.'

Tanner wanted to laugh. He was being paid for babysitting this egocentric maniac. The job had seemed at first fairly straightforward. The more he saw of Gilmour the more he realised there was a lot he didn't know or understand about his charge. There was a point at which he could surely assert his power and take the American back to town where someone else could take care of him. The look in Gilmour's eyes told Tanner that he would not be easily deterred, though.

'You've done this kind of thing before, I take it. This observing thing.'

'I told you I have some experience.'

'Where was that?' asked Tanner.

Gilmour wiped a hand across his brow. 'That was a long time ago.'

Through the netting walls of the tent Tanner could see Hays and Whitman discussing some detail of their evacuation. Gilmour had gone back to his maps so Tanner took the opportunity and joined the other two men outside.

'You made your mind up yet?' asked Whitman.

'I'm staying,' said Tanner, 'but don't ask me why.'

'Why?' asked Whitman obstinately.

'I don't want to go back just yet, I suppose,' said Tanner. The two men looked back to where Gilmour sat hunched over his table scribbling in his notebooks.

'I can't advise you to stay on,' said Hays. 'My advice is for both of you to get on that plane tomorrow with us. As leader of this base . . .'

'Forget it, Gary,' Whitman cut him off. 'They got their minds made up, it seems.' He wiped his brow and slipped his sunglasses back on. 'Though for the life of me it makes absolutely no sense. I mean I love this place but I can tell when things are getting silly.'

Hays nodded in agreement. 'This is the end of it all. There won't be any more survey teams down here for a good while now.'

'No,' said Tanner.

Whitman picked up the packing case and indicated the second one with a nod of his head. 'Grab that, will you.' Tanner picked it up and they walked the two hundred yards or so to the landing strip, marked out by white-painted stones, and the single tree where they were collecting their things ready for the plane.

Sweating freely now, they sat down on the cases they'd just carried over.

'All the lab stuff we can carry. Can't afford to lose any of it,' said Whitman, explaining the contents.

'You could always just leave him here on his own, I guess,' said Whitman, passing a bottle of water across. Tanner sipped the warm water and shook his head.

'No, I couldn't really do that.' The warm breeze cooled the sweat on his face, making the shirt stick on his back.

'Besides,' he continued, 'it may not be all that bad. He wants to go west because he has some idea that there's a pattern to recent attacks.'

'You mean he wants to find these bandits?' Whitman was incredulous.

'Well, he hasn't got much hope of doing that, has he? I mean, in reality we won't have enough petrol for more than a straight drive through to the railhead.'

'Just stick him on a plane back to Khartoum when you get there.'

'Yeah, I will – I'll have had enough of him by then.'

Whitman shook his head. 'It's a hellish train ride back from there.'

'I know,' agreed Tanner, 'but it may be my last chance.'

'Yeah, well, here's to a quiet trip,' said Whitman, raising the water bottle.

'A quiet trip.'

The plane was late arriving the next day. By the time they got everything loaded up and the pilot was ready to go it was growing dark. Benjamin and Abraham dashed up the runway lighting beacons – petrol-soaked rags in bottle-necks.

'It is safer flying by night anyway,' the pilot told his waiting passengers. 'They're taking potshots at anything that moves these days.'

This pilot was not the same man who had flown them down. He was a Belgian, named Severin. He was a small man, with clipped hair and tight-boned face. A pilot by nature – one of those men who discard all the attractions of a settled life for the sake of their one true love: flying. They fly the crop dusters and the air taxis, living in nameless resthouses under assumed names and dubious circumstances. They come from all walks of life, low-level flying in the great tradition of the aviator and his machine. A male-dominated profession in which man and machine are linked by some intricate thread that overcomes the need for any other kind of relationship. Severin was probably an average case. In his late fifties, he had nowhere else to go. No family that would take him back or that he wished to go back to, anyway. So he flew through the seasons, made enough money and travelled back to Europe perhaps to get rid of the frustrations that accumulated living cooped up with twenty other pilots in a resthouse for six months at a time. It was a bit different with the air taxi business – he could afford to rent a house along with a couple of others, which meant there was a little more room.

Death was something they woke up with every morning. They told stories about the people sometimes caught in the field. They would suddenly stand up, too late for the pilot to turn, and were decapitated. The storytelling was part of the whole way of life: each one of them had a tale to beat the last one. Severin was talking about rockets now.

'Heat-seeking, you see, they come for the engine. So what you have to do . . .' he paused dramatically and his hands took up the tale. 'What you have to do is, turn and fly straight into the sun.' He shrugged. 'This confuses them, you see.'

'Tell me about it when we get to the other end,' muttered Whitman as he clambered through the hatch into the plane.

They were loaded up and ready to go. Whitman squinted myopically at his spectacles as he wiped the lenses clean with a handkerchief. He leaned out through the open door. 'Look me up when you get back to town.'

Tanner said he would, then the door was pulled shut and he stood back. The engine opened up and the draught kicked the dust into Tanner's eyes. The tail swung round and the frail-looking

Cessna careered down the flame-lit runway, lifting off into the sky. The twinkling lights vanished in the luminous night.

By morning Benjamin and Abraham had packed up their family and started to move. They were going back to their village, which lay to the north. Tanner watched them go, mother carrying baby as well as huge bundle. Children, everyone, carrying something. They had forty miles ahead of them.

FOURTEEN

Cranes stretch their wings and take off to fly over unfinished canal walls. The sand shakes itself free from their feet and the sun dries their feathers in the wind. The marshes are sleeping and the old wreck is beached among the brown mud and the crocodile grass. The trees hang their heads and listen.

The carbs were full of dirt and the engine was stalling and missing all the time. Tanner explained what he thought the problem was.

'We'll do whatever you think is right at this stage,' said Gilmour.

The village was no more than a cattle station, home to about a dozen people, an extended family from the Nuer. Tanner and Gilmour had been driving for just over half a day when they came across it. The track they were on was not marked on the map, according to Gilmour, neither was the village. Just a clump of trees strung together with a cow pen and a couple of huts.

Skinny dogs snapped and snarled round the car as Tanner pulled up. Gilmour stayed in the car as Tanner tried to ignore the dogs. There was the sound of a woman singing in one of the huts. An old string bed was slung under one of the trees where a skeleton-thin man sat up and looked over. He whistled to the dogs through toothless gums. The dogs paid no heed, though they were gradually running out of steam. The old man called out for Tanner to identify himself. Tanner greeted him in Arabic. The old man must have recognised the greeting, for he yelled over his shoulder. A small child appeared, a little girl in a ragged dress running barefoot chased by the dogs which she casually brushed away.

The girl vanished into one of the huts to emerge a few moments later dragging a man with her. The man, in his twenties, wore blue flared trousers and was buttoning up a shirt as he walked

130

purposefully over. On his feet he wore plastic sandals of the kind which are fashionable in the big cities. From the doorway behind him small faces of curious children gazed on the scene.

The young man was formal and polite, though there was a wariness which seemed to hang in the air all around. The man spoke English so Tanner switched and told his story. It was one they had decided was best, the closest to the truth. They had mislaid the road and were trying to get to the road that went to the railhead.

The man offered Tanner a seat on the bed where the old man lay. He turned and called for two women to bring another bed. He stood aside to let them through. The women hurried away.

'You speak English very well.'

The man smiled. 'I am a student at the University in Juba.'

'Really?' said Tanner 'What are you reading?'

'Agriculture,' said the man, who appeared more like a boy the more he spoke. Agriculture seemed to make some kind of sense. Tanner thought of the number of graduates sitting round unemployed in the capital because they were too highly qualified to fit into the job market. Too highly qualified or too highly priced, one of the two.

'There was a strike by the students and the University is closed down now,' continued the boy. His name, he said, was the one he was christened with: Daniel.

'They are always striking about one thing or another. They are never satisfied with what they have got, they always want more.'

The door to the Land Rover opened and Gilmour stepped out. The American stood and looked around him before coming across. Tanner accepted the jug of water that was offered.

'Your friend is from the government?' asked Daniel.

'No,' said Tanner. 'Why do you ask?'

Daniel apologised and then said, 'He seems uneasy.'

'He is a visitor to this country, from America. He hasn't been here very long.'

Gilmour walked into the shade of the big trees. He nodded in greeting to Daniel and the old man.

'How's it looking, Tanner?'

Tanner made the introductions. 'This is Daniel. We can stay as long as we need to.'

'Good,' said Gilmour. The faces peered round the doorway at the two strangers.

Tanner dug out some tins from the car to add to the evening meal. Daniel was reluctant but finally accepted them. The men ate together by the tree, the women serving the meal to them in a large blackened pot.

'There are no men left here. They have all gone.'

'You mean because of the fighting?'

'The war is breaking down the walls of this house. Its children are scattered like branches broken from a tree.' Daniel paused to pass tea to Gilmour. Tanner offered his cigarettes to the old man who took one carefully before passing back the packet.

'They go north in search of work, promising to send for their wives and children when the time is right. They are fleeing the slide into war which is their fate.' He waved a hand round the encroaching darkness, his face lit by the flames from the small fire.

'You cannot plant crops in a battlefield.'

The conversation tailed off. Gilmour was going to sleep in the Land Rover. Tanner accepted the bed offered him; he would sleep under the tree. Their hosts moved away into the shelter of their homes. Tanner collected his sleeping bag from the car.

'How long is it going to take you to get the engine fixed, Tanner?'

'It depends,' he replied, 'on how much is wrong with it. Shouldn't think more than a day, though.'

Gilmour nodded, drawing himself up to his full height. 'I don't want to spend any more time here than is absolutely necessary.'

'What's your rush, Gilmour? This country is in no hurry. So what's this need to race madcap across the land?'

'It's my job, Tanner. That's what I'm here for.'

'You could race round this country all your life and never find a thing. It's a huge place, Gilmour.'

'I'm aware of that.'

'Yeah, well, I'll take you as far as the railhead, then I'm taking the train back.'

'You should have gone back with Whitman and Hays if you felt like that.'

Tanner nodded, shutting the door behind him and starting back towards the trees. He stopped and turned back to face Gilmour.

'And what are you going to do when you find what you're looking for? What will you do if you come face to face with this rebel army?'

'I have no specific plan. I'll do what I think is best.'

Tanner was angry now. 'It's not your war, Gilmour, it's not your fight. It's theirs.' He pointed back at the sleeping huts. 'This is their life and their land, it's not for you to decide what's best for them.'

'Don't be naïve, Tanner. In this day and age there is no such thing as a domestic argument. We are all involved in one way or another.'

Tanner shook his head with incomprehension. 'Why don't you just go home, Gilmour? Go home before you start something.'

'You can't turn your back on things for ever Tanner – sooner or later things come round to look you in the eye. You can't run out every time it gets to be too much for you.'

Tanner could think of nothing more to say. He walked away towards the bed that had been given up for him.

They constructed a shelter using the canvas from a tent and some poles tied to the Land Rover so that Tanner could work in the shade. Children came and went and the dogs nosed around curiously while Tanner stripped the fuel system. Gilmour sat under the trees on a deckchair reading a paperback.

'He is your manager, is he?' asked Daniel in his classroom English.

'No,' said Tanner. 'I'm just giving him a ride.'

Daniel looked over at the figure in the deckchair.

'One of our boys came home a few days ago.'

Tanner put down the carburettor he was cleaning.

'He was working for a company looking for oil.'

Tanner sat down in the dirt next to the other man who handed him the rag he was looking for.

'What happened to this man?'

'He was wounded when the rebel soldiers came to close down the development programme.'

Tanner glanced over to where Gilmour was turning a page. The American was just out of earshot.

'Was he hurt, this man?'

Daniel clicked his tongue and trailed a hand through the dust.

'He wasn't hurt. They set fire to the lorries. There was a lot of fire and smoke but he escaped. It was the middle of the night when they came.'

'And where is he now, this man?'

Daniel nodded his head in the direction of the huts. 'He is here.'

'Why did you tell me this story, Daniel?'

'I told you because you are somehow part of this situation, and because I thought you may have come to look for this man.'

'But you still don't say why you told me.'

'I can trust you.'

Tanner picked up the carburettor again. 'Pass me that spanner, will you?'

'This one?'

'Yes.'

Daniel passed the spanner and Tanner fiddled for a moment.

'Listen, Daniel, don't mention what you said, what you just told me. Don't tell my friend Gilmour.'

'You don't trust him?' asked Daniel.

'It's just that the less he knows the easier my job will be,' said Tanner, turning back to his work and finishing the conversation.

Gilmour slept through the afternoon. Tanner cleaned out the air filter and the plugs. The sun was easing off as he finally pulled the hood down. He had checked and cleaned almost everything he could think of. If there was anything wrong with the car after this then it would probably turn out to be a serious problem.

Joining Gilmour under the big tree, he shook him awake.

'That's it. I've done all I can. She's ready to go whenever you are.'

'Right, right,' repeated Gilmour, rubbing the sleep from his eyes. He looked round in the failing light.

'Not much point in moving off straight away really. May as well make a fresh start in the morning.'

'I agree,' said Tanner, 'but once we set off I don't think we should hang around.'

'How do you mean?'

'I think there's something wrong with the coil and we haven't got the spare. If it goes we'll be stuck.' Tanner held out his hands and shrugged. 'So I mean it would make sense not to make any unnecessary detours, really.'

'I see,' said Gilmour, who did not look impressed by this news.

He leaned back his head and closed his eyes again.

'What is that thing, Daniel?'

'What thing?'

'That mound of earth over there – is it a grain store or something?'

It was roughly triangular in shape, tapering up to a point about ten feet high at the centre, and made of mud bricks.

'It's a pyramid.'

'Made of mud?'

'Yes,' Daniel smiled. 'It was built by a priest who used to live here. He was a local man though he had travelled extensively through the country, and to Egypt it seems. He had some idea that he was in touch with the ancient Egyptian gods.'

'What happened to him?'

'He left one day after a big fight with the tribe that lived here. He said that he would make rain and save them all from starvation. They laughed at him.'

Tanner stared at the crumbling sides of the monument. 'What happened then, Daniel?'

'He left. He went into the marshlands to "resurrect his kingdom" he said. No one ever saw him again.'

Daniel lifted the wooden board, that served as a door, out of the way and stood aside for Tanner to enter.

The inside of the pyramid was small and cramped for just two. They stood stooped at the centre of the structure. The air was dusty and smelled of age. The only light came through the doorway behind them and through tiny slits in the walls now filled with cobwebs.

'No one comes here any more, but no one can knock it down in case he comes back.'

'Or in case it disturbs something.'

Daniel shrugged apologetically. 'These people are still superstitious,' he said by way of an explanation.

'And you,' said Tanner, 'are you superstitious?'

'I am a scientist. I have no time for superstition.'

As Tanner's eyes became more accustomed to the dim light, he began to notice the walls. He moved closer to one, where his eyes could make out a series of drawings: figures painted in various shades of red and brown, heavy shading in charcoal. The sketches depicted tall people with unnaturally elongated bodies and narrow heads. Spidery figures and outlines of birds in full flight, details of their outspread wings down to the tips of the feathers. There were huge pictures of cattle, their long curved horns so lovingly and proudly carved by the Nuer people. The mural seemed a mixture of traditional scenes of life on the cattle stations among the tribes, and the visions from the man's imagination or perhaps scenes from his travels: dhows, boats seen in the northern stretches of the Nile; railways, a train that seemed to be running through the whole picture, a long dark engine with steam in a black cloud trailing behind. There were pictures of Anubis, jackal-headed, and Isis and Osiris, the great sun raft and the falcons.

Tanner was astounded. He turned and moved round the room till the whole picture blended into one blur of vision, yet it was made up of so many different, seemingly unconnected things.

'What does it mean?' he asked softly. He looked at Daniel who was sweating; they both were – there was no air in the room. He

136

wiped a hand across his brow. Daniel shrugged. 'I don't know. He was a crazy man, they say.'

The whole room had the pulse of a temple, a religious place. Tanner stood in silence and gazed again round the paintings. His eye was caught by a figure in a green landscape. It was drawn slightly larger than most of the others, as though the artist had attached a greater importance to his role. He held in his hands two objects: in the right hand the moon rested in his palm. The left hand was held up, palm open towards the sky. From the cupped palm, water flowed through the fingers, over the sides as though too much for the hand to hold.

'The Rainmaker,' said Tanner, indicating the figure.

'Yes,' replied Daniel, who seemed uncomfortable inside the shrine.

Tanner moved over to the wall and touched the figure. 'So he really believed that he could bring the rain and save the crops, then?'

'He was just an old priest. He thought that he had great powers.' Daniel shrugged noncommittally. 'Of course it is all superstitious nonsense.'

'And so he just left?'

In the dim light Tanner could see only the outline of Daniel's face. He couldn't make out his features in the gloom. Daniel continued with his story.

'He wasn't from this tribe originally. He appeared one day from nowhere and he enchanted everyone with his stories. People came from all around to hear the tales of his travels.' Daniel's voice was low and even as he went on. 'I was just a child at the time, though my grandfather told me later about this man. He was just an ordinary man, I think, but somewhere through his travels he had acquired a mystical air about him, so that by the time he came here they hailed him as a prophet.'

The pyramid was a dusty echo of the man's life and perhaps also a hint towards the premonition that drove him on.

'He never came back, then?' asked Tanner, taking his hand from the wall and finding that the paint had stained his fingers.

'He left and went into the marshlands and no one saw him

again.' Daniel scratched his head and yawned. 'The following day the heaviest rains ever seen arrived. It was a coincidence, you see, that they told him to leave when they did.' He paused before explaining. 'You see, they were like all people, impatient. When he was unable to produce the rain he had promised, they threw him out. They forced him to leave and . . .'

'Somehow from his leaving the rains came,' completed Tanner. Daniel was at the end of his tale and wanted to get out into the open air, away from the oppressive room.

'It's just a story,' he said in conclusion. 'A coincidence.'

Tanner followed Daniel to the entrance. His fingers were coated in the ochre paint from the walls and he rubbed them together to clear them. Wiping his fingers on the rag he carried, he dropped his fingerprints on the threshold.

'He was neither a priest nor a prophet,' said Daniel. 'He was an illusionist.'

They left in the morning, following Daniel's instructions as to how to get back to the main road ten miles away. Gilmour was still unclear as to where they were in relation to his maps. Tanner drove steadily through the open bush; they were heading for a ridge of high ground.

'Do you ever wonder what might have become of you if you had been born out here?'

Tanner looked across at Gilmour whose gaze was fixed out the window. It was an unexpected question. He slowed the car down to cross a large pothole.

'I mean, do you think there would be a really fundamental difference in our character if we had been brought into the world in a place such as this?'

Tanner shrugged finally. 'I don't know. You, we, are all shaped by our upbringing.'

Gilmour turned back to the window. 'Perhaps.' He paused as though unsure whether to go on. Finally he said, 'My father wasn't a rich man, but he did his best for us, you understand, in the circumstances.'

The American leaned forward and snapped the air vent closed as a cloud of dust swirled into the cab.

'He always said that being black should never be a handicap for us, that we should never let it interfere with what we wanted.' He looked across at Tanner. 'I can understand you wanting to retrace your roots to this country.' Gilmour paused again, fishing for words. 'We are brothers in that, I suppose. The need to feel a belonging . . .' His words tailed off.

Tanner drove in silence, listening perhaps for the first time to this strange man who seemed finally to be emerging from the mantle of discretion. Then as the journey continued the conversation lapsed and Gilmour resumed his map reading. Tanner leaned forward on the wheel. It would be dark in a couple of hours and they needed somewhere to stop for the night. If it went well they could be there the day after tomorrow.

'Hold it, Tanner.' Gilmour was grabbing Tanner's arm.

'What is it?'

'Pull over, pull over here and stop.'

Tanner pulled over. He jerked the car into neutral and looked towards where Gilmour was indicating with his hand. 'There, do you see it?'

Tanner reached over for the field glasses on the back seat.

'The smoke,' said Gilmour urgently. 'Do you see it?'

Tanner looked through the glasses. 'Smoke – all I can see is smoke.'

Gilmour was tapping nervously on the dashboard. 'Yeah, smoke. Here, let me see.' He took the glasses from Tanner and peered through himself.

'We have to get over there.'

'You're joking,' said Tanner. 'That's miles out of the way.'

Gilmour set down the glasses and turned on him.

'Look, Tanner, if you don't like it then get out and walk.'

The smoke in the distance was like a single finger beckoning. The wheel turned in Tanner's hands. The sand beneath the wheels was cracked and split, like open sores in the earth's flesh. The Land Rover bumped and kicked its way through the ruts. There was a rush of the ocean that hissed through the trees and the bush.

The sand could feel the pulse of his heart, thought Tanner as the wheel jumped in his hands.

'I can understand your anger. But I have to do this.'

Tanner didn't bother to answer.

The going was not good and it took them almost an hour before they came to a gully which lead down to the village. They decided that rather than risk taking the Land Rover down the steep side, they would leave the car and walk. The ground was soft and they slipped and stumbled down the gully towards the huts. Smoke came from the ruins of what may have been one or possibly two huts set closely together. The blackened remains were spread out in a circle of ashes. The light was fading now as Tanner and Gilmour approached the assembled crowd. The high-pitched sound of women wailing. Their mourning sound. What had looked like a burned-out log from a distance was in fact the charred remains of a human being, the huddled figure twisted by the heat and flame, the hands held up to the face in a final gesture of despair. The cry of the women went up as their men strode barefoot into the embers to clear away the ashes from around the body. They moved quickly through the smouldering ruins, calling to each other as they went.

'Find out what happened, Tanner.'

Tanner turned on Gilmour. 'Someone's died, Gilmour, somebody is dead. What more do you want?' He felt the American was to blame for the whole affair. It seemed as though Gilmour were somehow pushing him up against a wall. There was a sense of foreboding in the other man's presence.

A shout went up as one of the women lost control and ran screaming on to the glowing embers. The dead man was her husband. The crowd of women clutched each other and wailed. The men shouted to each other and a couple stepped forward, but only one man went to the woman. She didn't want to leave, throwing herself forward to embrace her dead husband. The young man struggled to hold her back. The smoke was still coming off the body. Her dress was catching fire, the flames licking around the hem. She scrabbled in an effort to hold on to the charred unrecognisable figure, and for an instant actually dragged the body to her. Then with a tearing sound the arm gave way and, screaming, she let go. Without thinking, Tanner stepped up and helped the man to carry her away. The woman, who was no older than seventeen, fought and flailed wildly as they struggled.

On the edge of the crowd an old woman rocked back and forward on her knees, eyes closed, as though saying a prayer. Tanner and the young man laid the girl down on the ground; her feet were burned and she had fainted. The women rushed forward and tended to her. There was little else to be done. Night was falling and small braziers burning charcoal appeared in the gathering darkness.

Tanner found his way back to where Gilmour was waiting. He was sitting alone watching the remains of the blaze. The crowd had dispersed and there was only a boy sitting watching the flickering glow of the dying embers. The two bodies had been placed in a nearby hut where the proper ceremonies would be initiated.

Gilmour stood up as Tanner came back.

'Well, what did you find out? What happened?'

Tanner's face was blackened from the smoke, his eyes hurt and he was tired. He had found an old man who was willing to tell him what had happened.

'There was a fight. Some boys from another tribe – Nuer. These people are Dinka.'

Gilmour leaned forward. 'There was a fight, then what?'

Tanner wiped a hand across his face. He asked for some water. Gilmour had the waterbag on his pack and he passed the bottle over.

'They are all armed, you see. The army or the rebels, either side, they hand out weapons, modern automatic weapons, rockets – they all think it's the best way of gaining allegiance, making the conflict a tribal thing rather than a political one. Then the people will be more willing to get involved.'

'So it's a tribal thing?' asked Gilmour.

'I didn't say that.' Tanner took another swig from the bottle. 'There have always been conflicts between these tribes, but this is more than that. They came here, five men all armed with guns.

141

They accused two of the men here of having attacked some of their brothers. There was a fight and the two men were shot.' Tanner raised a hand to the devastation that lay behind them. 'They set fire to their home just for good measure.'

They went back to the car. They sat round a small fire and ate a meal which Tanner heated up from tins they had with them. The fire threw shadows on the American's face. Tanner was aware of something having been released today. They had come off the route he had hoped they would stay with. The only route out of here. He now wanted more than anything to be rid of this man. Gilmour seemed so detached from everything. In the light of what he had seen today Tanner knew he could never understand men like Gilmour; and yet there was some trace of himself which he had glimpsed in the man's eyes: a spectre of the despair and isolation that was within him somewhere.

'Where did this attack take place?'

'What?'

'The one they had come to avenge, the attack they had come to avenge, where was it supposed to have happened?'

'Just a couple of miles from here.' He waved with his fork.

'East? They said it was east of here?'

'I don't remember,' replied Tanner. 'Does it matter?'

'Perhaps. I was just curious, that's all.' Gilmour was looking at his plate.

'What do you mean, "curious"?' Tanner put down his fork.

Gilmour shrugged. 'Curious, simply . . . curious. I mean we just happen to be coming along, right? And this thing, this . . . attack just happens to happen. I mean right here, it happens right here, where we are bound to see it.' Gilmour was leaning towards him, trying to impress the point. Tanner persisted in his enquiry.

'Why should that make a difference, that we happened to see it?'

'You just said it,' replied Gilmour sharply.

'What? What did I say?'

The smile stretched back across Gilmour's face. 'You just said

142

it: we just happened to see it. Don't you think that might mean something?'

'Like what?' Tanner watched in silence as Gilmour returned to the business of eating.

'Well,' he started, his mouth full. 'Perhaps it's a little more than coincidence.'

'If it's not coincidence, then what is it exactly?'

'I don't know what it is.'

'You don't?' Tanner caught the packet of cigarettes that Gilmour threw across. Gilmour shook his head. 'No, but I know what it means. It means that they knew we would be coming along here at this particular time.'

'Who? Who knew?'

'They, the band that destroyed the rig.' It was obvious to Gilmour, it seemed.

'You mean they're following us?' asked Tanner carefully.

Gilmour finally lit the cigarette he had been waving in the air, blowing smoke across the fire. 'We gotta look further than what meets the eye. You realise that.'

'They want us to get out,' surmised Tanner. 'They're trying to scare us off.'

'That's where I'd put my money,' nodded Gilmour.

Tanner leaned back into the shadows. 'Those people down there, in the village, they died because we didn't get on the plane with Whitman and Hays?'

'That's how I figure it.'

'I don't get it,' said Tanner. 'Why not just hit us?'

'I know as much about this thing as you do, Tanner. I'm just working on an hypothesis here.'

'You're saying that this killing was all done to warn us off, so why shouldn't they go right ahead and just wipe us out?'

'Maybe they'd rather keep us on the run,' reflected Gilmour – unconvincingly as far as Tanner was concerned. When he spoke his voice was lost in the thin woodsmoke.

'Maybe they don't want to risk killing both of us?'

'I don't follow,' said Gilmour, dismissing the case. 'Either way it works out that we're in the middle of this thing.'

Gilmour seemed to be trying to convince Tanner that he meant no harm. Tanner was confused; he needed time to think.

'It would seem to me that the best thing we can do is get out of here as fast as we can.'

'I can understand what you're saying, Tanner, I really can, man. I mean, what are we doing here, right?' Gilmour asked, helpless. There was a catch. 'I only wish it were as easy as that.'

'Why should it be anything but easy?'

Gilmour spoke as though he were explaining to a child. 'There are no such things as political motives any more, not purely political anyhow. I mean, there can't be many idealists left who haven't found themselves undermined by the bank teller, right? The political is determined by the economic, it has to be. It's about survival. We've all got to eat, right? There's got to be food on the table.'

Tanner didn't say a word so Gilmour carried on after a moment's pause. 'That's what this oil thing is about. It's not about politics, it's money, hard cash for whoever runs it out of here and that's real power. I don't have to tell you this. You know what I'm talking about.'

Tanner shook his head. 'I don't know what I'm doing here myself, so how would I have any idea what you're after?' He was expecting some sort of reply from Gilmour, but there was nothing to show he had even been heard. 'This war has nothing to do with me,' he finished.

'You surprise me, Tanner, you really do.'

Tanner got to his feet. He thought for a moment that he had said the wrong thing. He had let his guard down for a second. 'We simply can't afford to stay.'

'I know.'

'You mean you agree?'

'Of course I do,' said Gilmour sincerely. 'It's obvious, Tanner, we're aggravating the situation by being here. We can't stay.'

There seemed to be a change in Gilmour's manner that was a little too abrupt. There was a new confidence now that differed from the arrogance of the early stage of their acquaintance. It was as if Gilmour had realised that he needed Tanner on his side, working for and not against him. There was nothing now that mattered but that their own two-handed drama should reach a conclusion. The change in Gilmour's manner was a confirmation of the power in Tanner's hands. He realised suddenly that nothing could penetrate the isolation in which they were trapped together. He recognised that as a truth that had been there all alone beneath the surface, hinted at in the tension that had been with them ever since the first time they met.

'You agree with me?' he repeated.

'Tanner, all I'm concerned with is concluding my business and then getting out of here as soon as possible.'

The fire was dying down now and Tanner realised suddenly that he was tired.

'One more day,' whispered Gilmour. 'That's all I need, just one more day.'

Tanner gazed through the bleary glow. All he could make out was the brushstroke of shadow where the eyes should have been. Gilmour stood and yawned. He stepped past Tanner, clapping him lightly on the shoulder in the manner in which a brother might.

'It would be a shame after all to go all that way back without getting what I came for.' The smile was so familiar. He had won, this time.

Tanner slept uneasily. He seemed to fade in and out of a series of disconnected dreams, a jumble of confused overlapping images. He was reminded of the sensation of drowning, in sand. He remembered a journey that he had made about six months ago when their convoy had been joined by a doctor who was going west to join a medical team that ran a station out there. A short stout man with a German accent who talked incessantly. He was curious to know about the landscape they were passing through. He was an amateur geologist and he had read somewhere that once the whole area had been part of an immense expanse of shallow tropical seas and coral beaches. The comment brought about a debate on the theory and various details that did not mean anything to Tanner

145

and moreover did not interest him. The voices receded into a blurr and he drove on, gazing out through the open window. He could hear the roar of the tide across the dry bones of the land and he could feel the swell of the sea beneath his feet. He could hear the water sweeping out from under the vacant horizon swamping everything in its path. The flat world turned over on its belly. Mountains buried deep in the ground, and the desert as wide oceans. There would be nothing left when the flood came racing in across the stubborn rocks and the hard-baked sand, nothing to meet the eye but the open hollow skull of the sky.

Somewhere between the reels of forgotten dreams and the restless sleep, the fever returned. The same fever that had lain dormant in his body for months now, waiting, waiting perhaps for a moment such as this to emerge once again.

When he woke up Tanner found he had overslept. The sun was stretched into the sky and he felt as though he had a hangover. There was a sound from behind the Land Rover and Gilmour's sleeping bag was gone. He stood up and then sat down again quickly, feeling dizzy. His head felt swollen. He recognised the symptoms of the malaria.

He got dressed and moved round to get into the shade of the acacia tree they had camped by. A cluster of birds took off with his movement and vanished into dark specks in the sky. Gilmour was rummaging through the back of the truck. Tanner caught a flash of something metallic as Gilmour thrust it into the pocket of his shoulder bag, hastily straightening up. Something small and metallic, something the size of a handgun.

'Good morning,' breezed the American, holding out a mug of tea.

'Morning.'

Tanner didn't mention the gun. He didn't want to ask in case he was right.

'I feel good today. I feel ready for anything.' Gilmour was in high spirits. Tanner smiled lamely. He chewed sullenly on the biscuit Gilmour passed him. They sat on the tailboard of the Land

146

Rover with the back door open, out of the sun. The village below seemed quiet now. They could see the odd figure moving round, going about its daily jobs.

'Strange how things seem so much more placid in broad daylight.'

'Placid?' Tanner looked round at the quiet sky and the curl of smoke from a fire in the village, a gentle wispy smoke unlike the harsh paroxysm of the last evening. He was still thinking about it when Gilmour interrupted his thoughts.

'I've been thinking about our situation and I have revised my opinion.' He stood and moved a few paces away from Tanner. He looked down towards the now quiet village. He waved a hand towards it. 'These people have suffered enough, don't you think?' He paused. 'I mean, don't you find it incredible that in the face of everything that has been thrown in their faces they still have the strength, the dignity to stand up and continue with their lives?' He turned back to face Tanner. His voice had taken on the venerable tone of a statesman preaching to his disciples.

'That I find quite astounding.' He clenched his fist tightly. 'That, that power, that indomitable spirit. If that power can be harnessed, if it can be used, then can you imagine what feats are possible?'

'You're saying that these people have the power to save this land?' said Tanner.

'Or destroy it.'

'What is your part in all this, Gilmour? I mean, whose side are you on exactly?'

'I'm not on any side, Tanner. I'm like you, simply an onlooker. I'm here to observe and report on my findings.'

Tanner had his doubts, but there was little he could say. If Gilmour was being honest then he had nothing to worry about. If he wasn't, then there was nothing he could do at this stage. He began packing away things to get ready to go.

'Shall we make a move, then?'

'Tanner, I would like to follow this incident a little further.'

Tanner slammed the door shut and moved to go round to the driving cab. Gilmour blocked his way.

'What do you mean? Follow what up?' He was curious to know where this would lead. Gilmour hesitated as though not quite sure how to proceed.

'This attack on the village that we happened to run across – I would like to find out a little more.'

'How much more exactly?' asked Tanner.

'Come along, Tanner. I'm asking for your co-operation and I am hoping for your voluntary assistance. We are stuck here together and the sooner I get what I want the sooner we can go home.'

'I could just leave you here and go home myself, couldn't I?'

Gilmour was silent for a moment, watching Tanner. It wasn't clear from Tanner's tone just how serious he was. When he replied it was softly and carefully.

'You wouldn't do that.' He said it as though to remind Tanner of some aspect of himself that he seemed to have overlooked. Tanner knew that Gilmour was right.

They climbed into the cab. 'Which way, then?' asked Tanner.

'South, I believe, just straight through the village and then roughly south-east towards the river,' replied Gilmour, who was busy examining the maps.

Tanner started the engine and they dropped down the shallow cleft towards the village. There was no one in sight as they drove slowly through. On the outskirts they saw the figure of an old woman sitting alone under a tree. She was the only person they saw. A lame dog sat next to her, standing up when it heard the car and limping away. Gilmour was silent. Tanner too said nothing and they drove on.

They drove on into the afternoon. They passed another village soon after the first but again there was no one to be seen. An open stretch of small fields marked out in what might have been millet but was now only dust. They found the tracks of a lorry which seemed to interest Gilmour. He knelt in the dirt and examined them with a pocket rule. Tanner sat in the van and watched him. He was shaking in fits with the fever. Gilmour noticed when he returned.

'You don't look well, Tanner, what's wrong?' he asked.

'It's malaria, I think. I had it about a year ago.'

'I can drive if you like,' Gilmour suggested, but Tanner was reluctant to hand over the wheel.

'How far do you intend following this set of tracks?' he asked. He was feeling weak and he wanted to turn the car round before he lost any will to challenge Gilmour's ideas.

'For as long as it takes. I just need to get an idea of who we're dealing with.'

'It could be the army, you know. They must be round here somewhere,' suggested Tanner. Even as he spoke he could hear the note of absurdity in his own words.

'It's not the army, Tanner, we know that, don't we?' Gilmour dismissed the theory.

'What are you going to do if we run into them?'

'We're not going to run into them. We're just going to have a look at them, that's all, just a simple harmless look.' He explained as though talking to a child.

They stopped to refill the petrol tank from the jerrycans strapped to the roof.

'We haven't got enough petrol to race round in circles after these guys,' Tanner called from the back. 'You know that, don't you?'

'Tanner, do you know what? You remind me of a reluctant bridegroom on his way to a wedding – that's it, a shotgun wedding,' said Gilmour over his shoulder, without even turning to look. Tanner came back and climbed back into his seat.

'You're not scared?' said Gilmour with a hint of a taunt in his voice.

Tanner ignored the bait. 'A shotgun wedding? And you've got the shotgun, I suppose?'

Gilmour said nothing. Instead he just sat there staring straight ahead. The conclusion was obvious. Tanner had seen the gun and now he knew what it was for.

'You know,' Tanner began, 'sometimes I wonder how I got here. I mean, here to this country, sitting here in the middle of . . .' He looked round, but saw nothing but open ground, scrub, bushes, dry and thorny, 'wherever this might be. It doesn't really matter where, what matters is why, why am I here?' He was just talking, thinking out loud. He had almost forgotten that Gilmour was there. It was strange that he could not have thought of anybody else to whom he might have been able to speak so openly.

'You're here for the same reason I am, Tanner,' said Gilmour finally, turning away from the windscreen. 'There's nowhere else you can think of where you'd rather be.'

They started off again. After about fifteen minutes they came in sight of a collection of trees, a line of forest that slipped from the earth and grew in size as they drew closer. The river. Tanner swung the wheel and accelerated up the side of an embankment that ran parallel to the strip of forest. Through the thin foliage the dried loam of the river bed could be seen. This was a small tributary, one of the many that meandered through this plain. It was dry perhaps only once in seven years. The path of the river led from south-east to roughly north-west. They were driving towards the west right now. Tanner was going home.

'We've gone too far here,' said Gilmour. 'We need to cut down across the river – there was a place back there.'

Tanner ignored him.

'Turn around, Tanner, we've gone too far.'

'We've wasted enough time. We're going back,' said Tanner, keeping his eyes on the narrow ridge they were driving on.

'Don't do this, Tanner. I don't want to have to use force.'

Tanner laughed. 'Gilmour, just take it easy. You can file your report on what you've got. Besides, we don't have the petrol to go any further.'

'Turn it round, Tanner.' Something in his voice made Tanner look across. The gun was there of course, clutched in that big fist.

'Don't be silly, Gilmour, you're not going to use that thing. Put it away before you hurt yourself.' Tanner waved a hand towards the gun, or towards Gilmour. The American pushed him away and grabbed for the wheel. They struggled for perhaps a second. The front wheel hit a pothole and the whole car leapt off the rails. Tanner could hear someone shouting as the Land Rover began to roll and then he felt something hit his head.

FIFTEEN

Desolation. They come here to bind up the dead. In solemn numbers of shambling barefoot misery, through the fields that would otherwise have been, but are now instead entombed in the weary dust of neglect. The sun sears the lid off the skyline as they gather children into their arms. Waif-like with the open-eyed dreamy distance of those who no longer have anything to lose; the dreaming and the dead. They wrap them now, not in muslin or fine silk, but in rough sackcloth that might bear the name of an unfamiliar harbour or a shipping line perhaps. Sacking tied with old strands of hemp rope which cuts the skin, whose bones creak as the final knots are tightened. The mothers are ageless. They hold their heads to one side and rock back and forth in the embrace of the listless wind that slips through their fingers.

What of the rest?

Listen and you can hear them coming now, charging through the startled streets. The students and the activists are shaking their pamphlets; they are rioting in your cities, beneath your very eyes. They are concerned with their own details, they complain of the price of sugar and butter, of inflated economies. The speak of their frustrations, the jobs they were promised. For a moment perhaps inside the slick vestibules of power the tremors are felt. The dust raised by the heels of the hysterical hordes has perhaps infiltrated even into these rarefied air-conditioned altitudes. But the crowd passes by.

The echo of the voices becomes more distant and more blurred. Down the corridors the odour of despair and desperation clings to the walls, hangs from the window shutters like tattered drapes. The halls and rooms are empty. The architects of bureaucracy have all gone home in the crushed back seats of taxicabs. There is no one here to listen to the protest and even if there were, perhaps he might straighten his open-necked shirt and slip his sandals on to his sore feet and step over to pull the shutters closed to keep the noise out. It was after all none of his particular business. How could he be expected to solve the problems of so many different people?

151

Fresh graves lie strewn across the landscape, piles of awkward stone like the markers of so many misplaced paths.

When he opened his eyes Tanner found himself hanging upside-down through the broken window of the Land Rover. The car was on its top. There was a dripping sound from somewhere that could have been petrol or water. His neck was stiff and for a moment or two he could not remember what had happened. His weight was pinning him in place. He eased himself out through the window. He touched his head and his hand was suddenly sticky with blood. He crawled through the soft silty earth until he reached a tree, against which he rested his back. The Land Rover had torn a scar in the side of the embankment they had rolled down. A gash led down to its resting place on top of a fallen tree. The four wheels pointed at the fragments of sky visible through the trees. The roots would burst through the underside of the roof and gradually the inside would fill with soil and grass would grow through the wheels. All would return to the earth. Even if they could turn the thing back over between the two of them there was a good chance it wouldn't drive. His ankle hurt from where he must have twisted it in the crash. He wondered where Gilmour was. He turned his head to see a large lizard about a foot long twitch and vanish into the earth.

He had the idea that he'd been left here to die.

For some reason his mind turned back to the last time that he saw Nina.

'It's not as if we haven't given it much thought.'

'I've told you how I feel.'

'No.' Nina shook her head. 'You told me that you still love me.' The fan turned slowly above them as she paced the room. She turned to face him again.

'I don't think you ever really meant what you've told me,' she announced.

'You mean I'm lying. What can I do to convince you?'

152

'There is nothing you can do and nothing you can say.' She sat next to him on the bed. 'What could you say? I know you better than you know yourself. There's nothing you wouldn't say to try and convince me, but I would know that you didn't mean what you were saying.' She rested her hand on his arm. 'It's not your fault.'

She stood up, straightened her skirt and walked across the room.

'There's nothing for you to prove, there's nothing you can say.' She turned to face him again. 'You're too wrapped up in your own struggles. There's no room in your life for love. You're too busy looking for something else.'

He wanted to tell her again that he did love her; he wanted to tell her that he needed her more than anything in the world. He needed her strength to guide him, to keep all the thunder and the pain of the world just that much further away.

'Nina, there's no one in the . . .'

She broke him off. 'Don't even try to say it, it's ugly.'

'Look, I understand what you're saying, but things don't have to end like this.'

'If you understood love then we wouldn't be having this conversation.' She shrugged as if to ask why they were having the conversation at all. There was nothing more to say. Tanner stood up and went to the window. The green wooden slats of the shutters smelled of dust and decay, preservation. Down below in the courtyard, the sound of footsteps came respectfully through the garden's early-morning slumber. A man carrying a straw basket full of leaves and a long wooden rake stepped up to the edge of the lawn. He was an old man with a permanent stoop bent into his back. On his head he wore a small orange skull cap that fitted his round head perfectly, a small crown of short grey hairs showing round the edges. Tanner watched the gardener as he paused like the devout reaching the gates of the mosque. He slipped off his worn leather sandals and stepped on to the lawn as though entering holy ground.

They agreed that this should be the last time they saw each other for a while. They both knew that in a matter of weeks Nina would be leaving for Venezuela, and in a few days Tanner was to fly south. They both knew that in all probability by the time he returned she would be gone.

'There's no more reason for me to stay here.' Her voice brought him back to the room. 'I want to go back home to my family.' He said nothing and she carried on.' I want to be someplace where everybody is speaking Spanish. I'm tired of travelling, tired of seeing so much sadness, so much that I can do nothing about.'

'But I thought you believed in this work. You've done so much good work, you've told me so.'

She dismissed his comment with a wave of the hand. 'It's nothing. Peanuts is what we are doing here. I no longer believe that I can save the world. All we are doing is running round the edge of an ocean trying to stop the flood with our bandages.'

Her gaze fell on something through the open doorway. 'We are just running around in circles trying to pretend that the big dark ocean isn't there. But it won't stop, it won't go away until they stop their wars and their stupid fighting.'

'So what are you going to do?'

She shrugged and sipped her tea. 'I need to rest. I'll go and live with my mother for a while. I don't know, I just feel very tired right now.' She looked at him for a moment, then she turned her head and looked out the window.

When he opened his eyes it was dark. He was cold and uncomfortable. He blinked his eyes and turned his head slowly, careful not to wrench his neck. There was nothing moving, though he could hear the forest breathing. Then the sound of feet coming through the undergrowth and the dancing flicker of the flashlight beam. Gilmour knelt down.

'Can you hear me?'

'Yes.'

'Do you feel strong enough to move:'

'Is it far?'

'No.' Pause. 'I'll help you.'

Tanner sat up and Gilmour helped him to his feet. He felt dizzy

154

and his legs were weak. Gilmour held him with an arm across his shoulders. They moved off slowly with Gilmour stopping every few paces to check his bearings with the flashlight, or to adjust Tanner's position.

'Why weren't you hurt?'

'I jumped clear,' said Gilmour. 'Instinct, I guess. I've got a couple of bruises and a few scratches, that's all.'

They stepped across a fallen log. The route was dropping downwards all the time. Suddenly they were out of the trees. There was a short descent down a small bank. They were on the edge of a huge flat mud plain. In the clear night the lopsided quarter moon lit up the landscape with a pale glow that shone in the hard crusty mud beneath their feet. Like a blanket of obsidian the mud covered the horizon.

'Where are we?'

'This is the river.'

The dried-out river bed stretched out in a layer of baked silt ahead of them. There was nothing moving in the shadows. They left the trees behind and shuffled through the dust.

'There's water here,' said Gilmour. 'All you have to do is dig down a foot or so.'

They rounded a bend in the river. They had been walking for a good half-hour when Tanner could just make out a low squat shape in the distance. They walked a little slower, for he was starting to tire. As they drew nearer he could see that the flat-shaped object was in fact a boat, an old paddle steamer or the remains of one. The big paddle wheel at the back was distinctive. The sky was deep blue, the colour of slate. The sound of an owl or some other nocturnal bird drifted across the ground from the treeline. Tanner sat down for a few moments' rest.

It took another fifteen minutes to get close. In the moonlight the low hulk of the ship was brooding and mysterious.

'We can rest and recuperate here while we decide what to do next,' said Gilmour.

The deck of the boat slanted down at the front so that it was possible with just a small step to get on to the lower deck. Gilmour went first. He turned round to Tanner, who had not moved.

155

'Well, come on, there's nothing to be afraid of.' He held out a hand. Tanner reached out and Gilmour helped him up on to the deck beside him.

'Are you sure it's safe?' asked Tanner. The boat looked old and most of the woodwork would have rotted.

'They made these things to last – most of the superstructure is steel.'

There was a sound from above and a dog-sized animal scurried away.

'Jackal or a wild dog,' said Gilmour, switching on his flashlight in time to get a glimpse of a pair of hind legs vanishing off into the night. 'Jackal.'

He led the way to the rear stairs which were steel and still intact. 'I let off a shot earlier, got rid of most of the residents.'

The whole boat stank of dead fish and bird shit. There were bones littered across the bottom of the stairwell. The paddle wheel was visible now; the wooden battens had dropped out leaving only the skeleton wheel frame: the great arched bones holding up the moon.

The room was small, the only one that still had a door to it. The room opened as all the others did directly on to the promenade that ran around the whole upper deck.

Inside, Gilmour had already carried one pack full of his things. He had another small bag with him now. There were two beds against the walls. There was a sink but there were two gaping holes where the taps had been. The room smelled of cordite and kerosene. Tanner was exhausted. Gilmour lowered him to the nearest bunk. There was one window, a single porthole beside the door. The door was hanging off its hinges and most of it had in fact fallen apart. The main frame was still reparable and Gilmour had already started collecting bits of driftwood and fixing them in place.

'What time is it?'

'Two in the morning.'

'That late? I must have been out for hours.'

'You were.'

The bunk was hard and the sleeping roll smelled of months of unwashed use. Tanner was too tired to care. His head was still hurting.

'All I have is aspirin.'

Tanner took two, swallowing them down with tepid water, then he closed his eyes and let his head fall back into the small bag that was his pillow. His leg ached where he had hurt it in the accident. His mind began to drift and he floated off down the dead river steered by eagles and towed by swimming jackals.

He was in the shadow of the high walls of a fort. Dervishes were spinning in the flames from a huge fire, their swords whirling the dancing light into intricate halos of electricity that hurtled off into the surrounding darkness. The shattered night glared down through the distant waning stars as the wind howled through the restless heels of the swordmen. People had come from miles away to be here and he could feel their relief as he passed through them. They could not speak to him and they could not hear his words but somehow he could feel their sorrow. They were waiting for something to happen. They had come here because they had no choice and now they were waiting to be allowed to leave. There was not enough water in the well. Enough for a short time, perhaps a few more days, but not enough for all of them for ever. Why were they dancing then? He wanted to ask someone, so he pushed through the crowds. He noticed that some of these people had lost their hands, some their feet. Some had died long ago; there were only dark empty sockets where their eyes should have been. He pushed through only to realise that the darkness was building up behind him, the fire was fading, leaving the dark walls round him.

The room was dim and cool as Tanner lay staring up through the gloom at the ceiling. He had woken up because there was someone in the room with him. He tried to turn his head but he was too tired even to do that. There was the sound of feet, bare dusty feet across the floor. The air smelt of moist earth as though the walls were made of mud. It overpowered him, suffocating him as though he had been buried alive. For a second his heart jumped and he lay without moving.

'Who is it?' he thought he heard himself say.

The Prophet was a tall man, well over six feet, and thin as a rake. Long hair plaited into locks with beads and feathers thrown in here and there. He wore a pair of tattered drill shorts and the remains of a shirt without sleeves or buttons. His chest was dotted with patterns like tattoos. On his left arm he wore a strip of leopard skin as an amulet high above the elbow.

He never stood still – he just moved round the room like a shadow. The lantern threw shifting pictures of coloured sand on the ceiling and shadows where his lean bony shoulders hung.

The sound of birds somewhere outside reminded Tanner that he had been thinking about the last time he saw Nina. He could see her now all tangled up in the bed, a mess of white cotton and that long black Spanish hair.

The man in the room was his father. He was dressed in the same donkey jacket. He looked just the same. In his hand he held a book. A large manuscript bound in leather with faded covers and yellowed pages. His father had once read him a story as a boy. He held out his hand to push the book away. It was filled with scrawls and curves of Arabic that made no sense to him. It wasn't that he didn't want the book, but that he couldn't read the words.

The man that looked like his father stepped back out of the light. He took off his hat and coat and he was the same man that he'd glimpsed before. The Prophet with his beads and his tattoo.

'You are wondering, perhaps, but I am the same as you,' said the Prophet, stroking the straggly beard on his chin. 'I am also, like you, the result of a split in direction. Opposite ends of a compass joined for one fateful night. That is where the secret of my – and of course your – power comes from. You are both North and South at the same time.' The figure of the Prophet scratched at his louse-ridden hair and smiled before going on. 'My father was a royal of course, descendant of the Nubian Pharaohs, the kings of Napata.' He waved a hand absently as though to express his desire to get over the preliminaries as quickly as possible. 'My mother was perhaps a servant girl, a slave who eventually died in chains for her sins. Those were big days for slaves. People say things have changed since then, but I see no evidence of that.'

He seemed to read Tanner's mind. 'I am older than you could imagine, though on the other hand I don't always feel that old.' He smiled ruefully. His eyes glazed over. 'This war is the same war all over again. I have seen it so many times. It keeps coming back.' Holograms appeared on the walls. 'Is it that mankind is destined to end up face down in the mud? Look at this place. Millions of years of evolution haven't changed it all that much. You can smell the bones through the earth. You and I have returned to the blood and placenta at the core of time.' Through the fingers of lantern light movement stirred kaleidoscope surges that blended into the sulphur glow.

'There has always been persecution of one kind by another; one brother hates the other. This country is not unique, don't you believe it – they have been killing each other for years, centuries and even longer. Yes, even here in this godforsaken land. The land of the blacks they called it, and they say when God created it he laughed. You can still hear his laugh if you listen to the dry wind coming across the cracked earth and the stones. The thorn bushes rustle with his mirth. A land fit for lizards and jackals.' The Prophet coughed to clear his throat, a dry drawn-out rasp. Bracelets jangled as he rolled another of his long brown cigarillos.

'I lose track of where I am.' He paused. 'Think of the Fur and the Beja, and the Shilluk and the Nuer and the Dinka, and all the others. All of them lived down here fighting among themselves, stealing each other's cattle and women. Things haven't changed much in that sense. Now they call themselves Marxists or Democrats and they align themselves with one side of the power struggle or the other. The fundamentalists are the worst of the lot; they think they are on the side of the almighty which means there's no stopping them.' He shook his head. 'Hypocrites, every one of them. I've never claimed to understand them.

'Don't tell me that you don't know what I'm talking about: the universal destruction of man by his brother man. You've seen it – all those petrol bombings of Asians living in the East End. You've seen it on the evening news, the stabbings and the muggings, all those things under the name of white man's superiority. While across the Irish Sea it's in the name of God, one religion versus the other. You've seen all of that and yet you feel you had to make this journey all the way out here to understand something that was pressed against your nose.' He sucked on the smoke. 'Travel is nothing but an illusion; it's all the same wherever you go. I used to think differently but I was younger then, or perhaps I was older; I thought I was wiser than my years. You see, it's all the same. All over the world they find the excuse time and again to annihilate each other. You don't need to travel to understand the horrors of war, you need go no further than your own mind to understand the holocaust, the incineration of six million burned like so many rag dolls, starved into submission. That is a crime; to forget in this day and age is a crime. Yet it will happen again; they are burning them alive in cattle trucks today in the west where the tribes sought to assert their identity among each other. All you have to do is close your eyes to hear the screams of all those dying people – men, women and children. Did they deserve to die? No, they did not.

'Of course now we have science to help us understand ourselves and expand our minds. Do you know which branch of science has made the least advances in the last hundred years? The under-standing of our consciousness. Sure we can fly monkeys to the moon and send cameras to Mars and even build bombs that will wipe out the entire earth at the turn of a key, but we still don't have any greater awareness of ourselves than we did over two thousand years ago. The Taoist priests had a better idea of what was going on than we do today. They knew the earth was round. They knew about Armageddon.'

Through the smoke that drifted in curls towards the ceiling, figures began to emerge. The sound of rotors chopping the tree tops outside, the whine of shells and the scream of planes. The sting of napalm and the groan of bodies hitting the ground for the last time. Whole forests wiped clear by chemical conspiracy. Out of the grey sea of mud in which Tanner found himself lost, bodies floated to the surface, their faces contorted by the last agony and the knowing.

'There is a final understanding that comes to us all in the last minute of life, the very last instant in which we see everything, but by then of course it is too late.'

The darkness and the silence of the room were familiar. Nothing was moving in here, nothing at all save for his breathing. The sounds and the pictures had receded, the light had gone down. Outside it must be dark.

They sent a train with all the food that would be needed to save them from the famine and the drought. While the city people argued as to whether or not the facts were to be believed, they sent a train. Long black plume of smoke across the burning horizon. Single track that nailed down the desert for thousands of mile upon mile. Long black train chasing night away from the day.

'This war has been going on since independence.' The cigar smoke drifted through the air. 'I have done my part, I have made my mistakes. I fought the British, you know.' He nodded now, smiling. 'I was there in 1924. I was another hot-blooded revolutionary. The whole continent was in flames. I wanted freedom. There was a reason to go to the grave. I'm not talking about all that nonsense about heaven and a place in paradise for those who die in battle – that stuff is for the birds, you can take it or leave it as far as I'm concerned. In the bloody state of fear and misery that is war, there is nothing save your own wits that can pull you through alive, or sane. I've seen those boys die with a prayer still warm on their lips. I saw them cut in half by the bullets, torn limb from limb by shrapnel and explosive. Being wounded was no relief either. If you think the hospitals are bad now, you should have seen the ones we had in those days. The wounded all too often wished they had received a swift death in the heat of battle rather than endure the long stinking slow gangrenous death that awaited them in the field hospitals.'

The teeth gleamed in the light. 'That's when I decided that I

161

was no hero. I knew that instantly. Freedom was worth dying for, they said. Throw the British out and we can live as we please. So we got rid of the British, or rather they finally conceded to inevitability and we gained independence. So what did we do then? We started fighting among ourselves. Freedom is never simple.'

He raised his arms wide. 'A quarter of a continent embraced as one nation, and we couldn't do it. No surprise, I suppose. Now the real war is the bribery and corruption, the deals that turn the wheels, my boy. It's all over the place, but people are too busy fighting each other to even have time to worry about it; they just accept it.' He raised his eyebrows laconically. 'I suppose everyone has to protect their own interests. What chance have the children got in a world that promotes fanaticism as a means of survival?' He paused and leaned forward until his breath was in Tanner's face, the stink of foul tobacco and stale whisky. 'I tell you this because I was there, I saw it all.'

The voice fades in and out of focus. On the screen that is the wall or even the ceiling perhaps, a scenario unfolds. Dark figures in long coats, in a landscape of barbed wire and mud. The skyline is scarred by the orange sodium flame of destruction which is taking place on another battlefield somewhere. The figures are moving slowly through the smoke. Long coats covered in blood and earth. The figures are tall and thin, weighed down by the mud which grips their boots, making it almost impossible to move. There is no purpose in their movement – they move as though driven by something which has ceased to have meaning. As they get closer it is clear that their faces are covered. They have huge swollen eyes of glass; they wear rubber masks, gas masks. Yellow mustard gas drifts in plumes across the bleak landscape. Grotesque skeleton men whose skin is the colour of ash and the texture of paper lie in the prolonged agony of death, fingers scrabbling for a grip on the fast-fading light.

'I don't have to justify what I've seen.' He paused. 'You see,' he began again, 'you and I are similar in that we were both born out of opposites, the coming together of differences. We are both born of integration. That is the only solution.'

162

The man pushed back his braided hair. 'The other way holds nothing but destruction, I was there in '24, a minor affair, but I was also there when they removed Gordon's head from his shoulders in the name of freedom. That led to the worst famines you could imagine. But more than that I saw the soldiers at Verdun so drunk they had to be carried to their posts. I saw the children burnt into shadows at Hiroshima. Only man could be so cruel as to devise such methods. God has nothing to do with it, it was out of his hands a long time ago.

'I don't have to justify what I've said. Your poets have been silenced and your freedom has been thrown back in your face. I have seen all this, I was there.' He paused a moment. 'But where were you?'

Where were you?

North.

In the quiet offices of the government, under the gaze of luxuriant palm trees nothing was stirring. The ceiling fans and the doors stood open, telephones rang, their shrill tones echoed down empty hallways, but no one ever picked them up. Gaze out across the slow easy sway of the river and see that nothing has changed. On the evening verandas the wealthy assemble to discuss the politics and the rumours.

—These things have been happening for centuries.

—They go in cycles, you know, seven years.

—Seven years of life and seven years of dying.

—It's all to do with nature.

—I blame the Soviets.

—This war would have been resolved a long time ago if not for them.

—Things are always made to sound worse than they really are.

—It's called propaganda.

—I was there.

In the shanty towns on the south side of the city the refugees assemble with nowhere left to go. They left behind their homes and their cattle have been stolen or lost in the fighting. They have no choice; you cannot tend to crops when there is a war going on around you. They have no water here in this cardboard village. They have no jobs. They have to pay for the water; five times the price anyone else would have to pay.

The palace walls are crumbling into the dust and the beggar boys run through the market place chasing the lepers. The old men gaze from the tea shops and the storytellers gather their crowds. The sharp moustaches settle their deals and the crooks stay away from the sunlight. The conspirators gather to make plans behind the the mosques. The taxi drivers overcharge the foreign girls and they sleep by the river all day. Nothing ever happens here and everyone's up to one scam or another. The Eritreans pluck their hair with long wooden combs and talk of war. Crippled by hatred, they struggle on in their journey north to the confluence of streams.

The thin silver blade moved, a carefully measured pace across silver satin expanse. The movement was seconds into minutes into miles; years turned into light. Slowly coming awake. The golden-brown black hairs nuzzled against the sunbeam-draped copper yellow across his arm. He saw a mark on his arm that he hadn't seen before. The scar on his wrist was like a chain of smoke-ringed mountains that he'd seen in a film somewhere. The silver blade twisted and turned regardless of wind and stars. The tiny blue vein that carried his pulse beat gently against the leather strap.

It was quiet now, the room was still.

A face appeared that was vaguely familiar. Tanner rolled and tried to stand. Hands reached out to steady him; he had to sit down again straight away before he fell.

'Easy, boy, easy.' The hands set him back.

The face was familiar but it had changed. Tanner had forgotten the name.

'It's me, Charlie, Charlie Gilmour, remember?'

The red eyes and the grey whiskers were unfamiliar but the name brought it back. Gilmour held out a bottle. 'Here, try and drink some water.'

Tanner sipped from the water, though it tasted bad. He wondered if it was him or the water that wasn't right.

'How do you feel?'

164

'How long have I been out?'

'Three days – at least I mean you've been in and out of it.'

'I had malaria once before,' said Tanner. 'You never get rid of it.'

Gilmour sat down next to him, and held his head while he drank again. The water came back and he retched violently. Gilmour cleaned him up and set him back, then he leaned down until he was close enough to whisper.

'They're here.' His voice was high and excited. 'They're here,' he repeated. 'I've seen them.'

'Who?' said Tanner. 'Who's here?'

'They are, I told you I've seen them.' He pointed towards the doorway. Tanner's head ached and he could hardly think straight. The American smelled of stale sweat and unwashed clothes.

'There was someone else in the room.'

Gilmour's eyes widened. 'In here? No.' He shook his head from side to side. 'There's no one here but me and you.' He was silent for a moment. Tanner looked at him and then round the room. There was no one else there, it was true. Gilmour was pointing at the window again.

'Out there, they're outside.'

Tanner shook his head. 'No, I heard voices in here, someone was talking to me.'

'Out there.' Gilmour inclined his head and smiled in the bad light. He held his field glasses to his eyes. Tanner swung his legs off the bunk and tried to stand. The sound of him falling caused Gilmour to turn on him. 'Quiet!' he hissed. Tanner pulled himself back up to the bunk, sitting with his head down between his knees. He breathed deeply. He realised that he was scared. He was scared of being out here alone, scared of being too sick to move and more than anything perhaps at this point he was scared of his companion.

'What is it you're looking at?' he asked slowly.

'A group, five . . . no, six men; troops wearing an assortment of colours. Different outfits and an array of weaponry.' Gilmour spoke without taking his eyes from the lenses of his field glasses.

'Then we'd better just sit tight and hope they go away,' said

Tanner, stating his words carefully, tentatively as though he expected to be interrupted at any moment.

'Here, look.' Gilmour held the glasses for Tanner to take. Tanner stood and took a step forward. He held the glasses up and leaned against the window.

Out under the spiral of night a fire was burning some distance away. Possibly on the river bed itself about half a mile away. He saw the glimmer of the fire and the figures moving through the troubled darkness. A handful of people standing round.

'Probably a small independent unit of the rebel forces. They act alone on their own initiative. Attacking wherever they think fit.'

Tanner put down the glasses and turned to look at Gilmour again. The American was rummaging through his rucksack. He picked up his camera and checked the film and reached inside again.

'What are you doing?'

There was no reply, Gilmour continued as though he hadn't heard him. Tanner stepped closer and leaned his face into Gilmour's, almost touching him.

'What are you doing?' he repeated, stepping back as he spoke. Gilmour stopped what he was doing and sat and regarded Tanner carefully.

'I'm going down there to get a closer look.'

'Down there?' Tanner leaned against the window. 'I don't understand. What for?'

Gilmour stood up and pulled the straps shut on his bag. Talking as he went, he reached inside his small bag and produced the oily rag Tanner had seen that morning at the village and again just before they tipped over the side in the Land Rover.

'What are you going to do with that thing?' The revolver.

'I'm going to follow them for a day or two – maybe more – so that I can find out exactly what they are doing, how they're operating.'

'This makes no sense. Who are you working for?'

'Between you and me, Tanner, does it really matter who I'm working for?'

166

'No, I suppose it doesn't. You're not working for one side or the other. Is that it?'

Gilmour sat down on the bunk and stared across at Tanner who was slumped to the floor, his back propped against the wall. The room was warmer, it seemed. The stars had been covered away for the night.

'I don't have to justify my actions,' Gilmour began. 'You might think that we are all responsible for our own behaviour, everything that we do, from the minute we're born until the moment we die, every single thing we do, every decision we take is ours and we must take the responsibility for the consequences, but is that really the case any more? Things are all tied up together. Everything we do can be explained in terms of the actions of those around us. For the most part we all fumble along following the route of least resistance. What happens when things go wrong? We blame those around us, because we were following them and therefore how could we be expected not to make a wrong turn? External factors, the eternal process of shifting the blame.'

'That's not true.'

'Of course not,' smiled Gilmour with the gleam in his eye of the patient hunter who has finally succeeded in luring his prey to the bait and may now savour those final kicking struggling desperate moments as he takes his aim. 'Of course not,' he breathed. 'But we don't have to look too far for an example, do we? Take yourself – you, a man of integrity, good intention, honesty?' His head jerked forward. 'You're nothing but a small-time confidence trickster. I've known that since the first time I set eyes on you. That's why you hate me so much, isn't it?' Gilmour smiled in the bleak flickering light. 'You with your high and mighty half-caste morality. You could never step off that pedestal even to save your own life. You try to deceive everybody but most of all you're deceiving yourself. You don't fit in because you don't want to fit in, because it makes you feel special.' He almost spat the words out. Tanner heard his voice as it spread through the room like oil on clear water. 'Your empathy for the people of this country is nothing but an empty-headed dream.'

'That's not true.' Tanner's voice wavered. 'You don't know me,

Gilmour. You never could.' His voice shook with an excitement that lay somewhere between fury and fear.

'Don't I? Well, then, tell me something, Tanner. What are you doing here? Here in the middle of this whole mess? Do you really know why you're here? Is this where your real self lies? Or is it that you couldn't stand what you had become – a second-rate nothing, so you left. What were you before you came here?' He raised a hand, 'No, don't bother trying. I'll tell you. You were nobody, you even bribed your way into this limp excuse of a job through a crook your father used to know.' Gilmour pointed with his finger now. 'You are a part of the very thing you profess to hate; the corruption that's bringing this country down. So don't get self-righteous with me.'

Gilmour turned back to his packing. Tanner lifted himself to his feet. His body was shaking and he leaned his head back against the steel wall. He felt dizzy and light-headed despite moving slowly and carefully. He could feel the rush of air from the door on his shoulder.

'What are you going to do now?' he asked.

'I'm going down there and joining those boys.'

'You're mad.'

'Perhaps to you but that's what I'm here for. I've made contact with them so now I shall go down and offer my services.'

'So you're a soldier, then, but whose side are you on?'

'I'm not on any side, Tanner. I represent certain interests whose wish is to maintain the instability of this area. You see, the power struggle could go either way in this country, and my people are concerned that when it's all over they retain a certain favoured position. Does that make any sense to you?'

'What about the oil?'

'Exactly, Tanner. What about the oil? If there is any, and there will be, then we'll have a controlling interest.'

'So the fighting has to go on.'

'That's what I'm here for. It's a small fight on the global scale, but every war is won through its minor battles. I'm here to instil confusion, to sow the seeds of discontent, as it were, but in the right places.'

168

'I don't understand,' said Tanner, his voice not more than a whisper. 'How can you do that? How can you continue to perpetrate such violence? The killings, the death? How can you do that? It's not your country!' he hissed.

'No, and it's not yours either, Tanner, so don't start lecturing me on morals.' He pushed Tanner back against the wall. Then he eased his grip of Tanner's shirt and stepped back a pace. He seemed to wait for a second for the moment of anger to pass. 'Your problem is that you'll never understand, Tanner. The world is divided into those who take part and those who stand around and watch, and believe me, Tanner, you're not the type to act. There's not a bone in your body. So don't start blaming me for my convictions.'

Gilmour turned and bent to pick up his bag. As he leaned forward Tanner pushed himself away from the wall with his hands. He crashed into Gilmour and they fell to the floor. Surprised, Gilmour hit his head on the metal bulkhead. Tanner's hand found the camera. He lifted it and crashed it into Gilmour's head. The pistol went off and the sound of the shot was deafening in the enclosed room, the metal reverberating. He felt the sharp burning pain as the bullet went into his thigh. The gun fell to the floor. Gilmour had stopped moving. Tanner heard himself shout out as he raised the camera again and again and smashed it into the back of Gilmour's skull.

'Enough, enough,' he cried, until finally he ran out of strength and fell back. Gilmour's body twitched once and then he was gone.

Out across the mudflat the flames burned untended through the night. The conspirators had fled into the welcome darkness.

Too late, it is all much too late. In the open tracts of the western desert the footsteps have long since ceased to echo through the unforgiving silence. The people are assembling from the shadows in numbers, arriving from all directions of necessity to find there is nothing left for charity to give. In the camps refugees huddle together and wait for fate to deliver them. In the markets the paltry gifts are priced and stacked. The grain silos lie empty; even the rats have moved out. The people are on their knees once more and the airlifts are grounded. The relief train lies broken-backed at the bottom of a windless ravine.

Dark convoys of lorries steal through the still motionless moments before dawn. The fighting will continue as long as there is ammunition to go round and guns to buy. The sides are already blurring as the casualities become personal. There is no final outcome, only sustained suffering is assured. The hope lies in the realisation that there is no longer any need for North or South, for East or West; it was never meant to be simple.

Perhaps it is already too late; habits once acquired are hard to break. Where to begin? Behind closed doors the women still mutilate their daughters in the ignorant confusion of propriety. The football crowds flock to the public mutilation of petty criminals. The foolish sacrificed for the peace of mind of the moral masses. Old women are flogged for brewing beer in tin tubs. Where in the midst of such confusion should we begin? There are rumours of slave-trade revivals and genocide. Scratch your name on the walls of the little palaces and bury your vengeance.

Within the walls of the city the children of the wealthy and the fortunate amble through the dusty booklined corridors of their ivory towers dreaming dreams of western escapism and religious salvation. The cobwebbed labyrinths of government where the sentry boxes are filled with sleeping guards. There are rumours of bribery and corruption. The portals of power are quiet and vacant. Occasionally the awkward sound of someone clearing his throat echoes down the weary hallways as one man steps down and the next leader takes to the stage with yet another empty promise poised on his lips. The question remains as to how long this can go on.

Meanwhile the streetboys lie senseless under parked cars, high on sniffing petrol and drinking stolen gin. The traders are all weeping for the black markets and the flea-ridden carcasses hanging from the meat hooks. It is the same everywhere. People seem to have forgotten that things don't have to be this way. The dogs lose their faith and run rabid through the streets waiting for someone to put them out of their pain.

SIXTEEN

The drumbeat tapped gentle and low, irregular like a nervous racing heartbeat. One minute the rhythm rose and fell, building at times into a huge rushing crescendo. The thunder rumbled across the troubled sky. Then the beat would begin to subside like a wave, tailing away slowly to an even fluttering roll.

The first drops hit the dry aching ground hard and heavy. The thirsty soil swallowed the water straight down, sucking the liquid eagerly through the pores of its parchment skin. The heaving rush went on and on until the surface was saturated and the rain began to splash gleefully into pools of mirrored delight that jumped and danced with each new drop's arrival.

In the half-light of dawn Tanner didn't recognise the sound at first. He had forgotten the sound of rain. Lying half-awake he heard the clatter beating on the roof above his head. He smelled the moist change in the air. He heard the whisper of water rushing through the trees and the swirling water that hung like a curtain from the deck of the boat. With a feeling almost of shock he realised what was happening.

Tanner tried to move, but it seemed his legs were rooted to the bunk. He raised his hand to his face. It was damp. He moved the hand down his body; the bedroll was damp and sticky. He raised his head and saw the dark patch that stretched from his waist almost to his feet. He pulled the cover away, wrenching the stiff cloth back. The flies buzzed violently at being disturbed. He sat up, his leg hurting. There was a haste now in his actions, like a drowning man struggling to deny his fate.

The bullet was buried in his leg, just above the left knee. He could just about stand on his leg for a moment if he kept his weight on the right leg. He tried to take a step and he fell face down across the body that lay in the doorway. Gilmour lay head first through the door. The room seemed to be drenched in blood. The buzz of flies filled Tanner's head as he felt his way to the open air.

Gilmour's head was almost unrecognisable; the broken remains of the cine camera lay strewn about. Two scraggy-looking vultures splayed their wings and fell back.

Tanner reached the rail and threw up over the side. His head was spinning, his body was cold with sweat. He waved a hand wildly at the scavengers. 'Go on, get out of here, go on.' The birds took off in a flurry of feathers, taking the unholy stench with them to the far end of the deck where they paced warily round each other. There would be others here soon; they were impatient to take advantage of their timely arrival.

Tears ran down his face as he dragged the body back into the cabin. The rain still splashed easily on the wooden railings and the steel decks. The water was seeping through the roof of the cabin, falling now in streams that poured through the ceiling. Everything was soaked in rainwater. He collapsed backwards until his back was against the wall, Gilmour's head in his lap. Through the doorway he could see the sheets of water, pale in blue-grey colours of the sky. He held one hand out to catch the water from the ceiling, running the other distractedly across his face. Tanner wondered when the rain had arrived. He let the water play in his outstretched hand; it had come while he was sleeping. The sky was a long band of unbroken troubled clouds. which had edged into the night, gently nudging their way in while he slept and dreamed of somewhere else. A solitary ray of sunlight burned a hole through the curtain, throwing rainbow shades that fell in an arc towards the softly drowning land.

The open sides of the river were already flooding. The rain seemed to wash all his worries away, if he just let himself go. If only everything were so simple, he thought, as he stared at the gleeful burlesque through the railings of the deck.

Tanner turned back to Gilmour's body which lay across the floor. Gilmour was dead and he was finally free. He wanted to jump and run naked through the rain. He tried to stand but his leg was too painful; it felt swollen and dull. Instead he crawled and staggered to the stairs, and down to the shelter of the lower veranda where he sat and watched the storm. The clouds thickened and the sky pressed down as the light grew fainter.

In front of him Tanner saw the ground move. He thought it must be a trick of the light somehow concocted by the splashing water and the grey darkness. But he saw another movement, then another. The ground was coming to life below his feet. The whole wide plain of mud that surrounded the boat was starting to shift and undulate. Flecks of mud spattered into the air. He leaned forward as far as he could without falling off the deck. There was another flurry of movement away to the right. There was a flash of silver. Somewhere in the distance a rumble of thunder. Then again the silver flash forced through. The rain still splashed down and now the whole plain was coming to life. The fish wriggled and squirmed, their scales throwing sparks in the dull light. The lung fish forced their way from the wet bleeding womb, covered in membrane and flecks of mud. They flipped their bodies, trying to move now in the direction of the river, which was itself swelling to offer itself. There were so many that he could not count, hundreds perhaps. The boat was buried in a living graveyard. These fish had dug into the mud when the river had retreated, forming a membrane coccoon and sleeping in hibernation. This ageless process had been going on since the first vertebrates lived on this planet over four hundred million years ago. They were here now, they had emerged here and now, thought Tanner. Perhaps they had slipped through the door of time, or perhaps he himself had slipped back into the Archaean depths of time.

It was warm and pleasant rain that seemed to fall today as Tanner sat and dreamed on the veranda of the stranded paddle boat. Upstairs the birds returned and squabbled to get through the door. His leg hurt and he needed to make some kind of splint to enable him to stand. He needed medical help and the longer he left it, the greater danger he was in. He stripped down a railing and with his knife cut it to size. Slumped back against the wall of the boat, he closed his eyes; he was exhausted. The river had widened through the morning from a trickle to a fair-sized stream. Soon the great torrents of water would come hurtling from the hills and the river would surge to full flow. He wondered what would happen to the home he had found. Would the boat perhaps lift out of the mud and float away downstream? In the Ganges they cast the ashes of the dead to the water. If he set light to the boat then the burning funeral pyre would carry him along until all was ashes and he would slip silently beneath the surface of the muddy swirl for ever. There were matches in the pocket of his shirt but they were damp and refused to catch.

The noise of the scavengers on the upper deck disturbed him and he made his way back up the stairs. The doorway was drenched in blood and alive with the beat of wings.

The pistol lay on the deck; he grabbed it, shouted and fired off a shot. The vultures and the crows took off in a flurry of sorry-looking feathers and blood-drenched claws. The stench from the cabin was appalling. Tanner had to hold his breath as he dragged the pack across the room. He tried not to look at the remains of Gilmour's mutilated body. The broken camera careered across the floor as he caught it with his bad foot.

The steps were slippery and wet and his leg hurt as he climbed carefully down. He had thought about burying Gilmour but he didn't have the strength to move the body.

Tanner wanted to leave. He dropped now the last feet to the flooded plain and his leg collapsed under him like a twig. He sprawled in the mud. He managed to lift up the pack and tucked the pistol in his belt. The rain had stopped for a while. All around his feet the fish continued in their struggle for life, dragging themselves from pool to limpid pool, always towards the river. Some didn't make it, too weak after their prolonged stay under-ground. They lay defeated in the mud. They would wriggle and kick and struggle to be free until one by one they gave in. Tanner staggered past and away into the sinking mud.

He had gone less than a hundred yards when he realised that he couldn't carry the heavy pack any further. He collapsed to the ground. It was starting to rain again and heavy drops ran through his hair and down his face. The straps came free and the pack fell away into the earth. The straps round his leg were loosening. He couldn't tell if he'd lost a lot of blood, but he felt at the back of his mind that he must have. He lay back in the stinking black mud which seemed to draw him in, like the warm embrace of death around his shoulders. He lay back and the sky seemed to rush by, whirling clouds spinning through the trees. He wondered if he would die here, and he would sink into the mud for ever.

He wondered if he would lose his leg.

In the underground hospitals carved into Abyssinian hills of mud and gold, they amputate the legs of young men and women by candlelight. Casualties from war. The hospitals are run by women and old men; everyone else is either fighting or starving. Anyone who has any skill at all is important here, any skill is born from desperation. The desperation of having the minimum in everything: facilities, equipment, qualified staff. The rebel armies, the freedom fighters, the revolutionaries – they all come here to die. They bring their wounded here by truck, by mule, by foot. The surgeon is no more than an orderly, but he has done this operation thousands of times. He wields the saw in the glow from the flickering flame, feeds the bone to the teeth. The wounded, from different wars but victims of the same disorder, lie side by side in the subterranean wards, but the rows of wooden arms and legs are identical. In the next room the crippled and the limbless sew flags together in silent penance, the wheels of the old Singer machines spinning like prayer wheels.

The thick grey trees that surrounded the river plain were dry and bare, kept alive by the water that lay buried here, underneath the floodplain. Water that retreated deeper into the earth by the day, away from light and life. The water had to be replenished annually if life was to go on, if the land was to survive. The plain was fed by rivers that swelled and broke their banks when the time came. The water flowed down from the high ground that lay to the west and the east of this bowl, and from the big rivers. The swamps would expand to eat up the forests and the open ground to form one huge expanse of channels and waterways. The reeds and the floating grass would flourish and everything would turn green. Two hundred miles in any direction. Once inside there was no way out. Thousands of tons of water rushed into this floating garden and vanished never to emerge. The rivers that led out went north, but thousands of tons were lost as though spirited down into the depths of the

175

planet through a huge duct that lay underneath. So it was said that once drowned here you would be sucked down by the pull of the water into a whirling bottomless maelstrom, into eternal damnation, into the abyss.

The torrent of rain falls upon the blistered land. Like a huge carpet, the band of cloud unfurls itself across the length of the country. The drops lick the surface of the parched soil as though it were the cracked lips of a man driven by thirst to desperation. The pummelling waves fall in time to the pleading wind.

The children dance in the cascade of tears, singing and laughing with all the innocence of joy. Muddy dogs snap at the flying heels and run in circles through hoops of rain.

The old trains come to a standstill on the outskirts of nowhere at all, between towns and villagers, between families and friends, between bends in the track. The driver wipes sweat from his brow as he shuts down the throttle lever and tugs on the steam whistle to let the passengers know of the delay. The great iron wheels roll over and come to a halt. The people stretch in their uncomfortable seats (those who have seats) and the men rise to help the women and children down the high step to the ground. The pool of water covers the track ahead and they will have to wait a day until it lowers itself enough for the train to cross.

In the city the cars gleam in their shiny new coats, washed clean by the storm. They move warily through the undrained streets which have been transformed overnight into overflowing rivers. They cruise by, throwing water over the Coptic priest who lifts up his skirts and tries to negotiate an awkward puddle in front of the church. He is in a hurry and he has just watched a young man use a half-brick that protrudes from the dull water as a stepping stone. He stretches out and his sandals give way, plunging him to his ankles in the water.

The air is fresh as though replaced temporarily or infused with oxygen. The schools are closed as no one can get to work. The orphan girls are playing in the damp streets making boats from bottle tops and bits of old wood.

In the farmlands the landowners walk through the fields telling jokes to the workers, giving thanks publicly to Allah for assisting them in making sure of their profits this year. Their plump faces spread wide with opulent smiles revealing the flash of gold teeth and the charm of a snake.

On the heels of the rainbow the people in the west know the rain is too late and too brief to be of any real significance; it is too late. They run in delirious circles nevertheless, to collect what they can in buckets, in old milk tins, anything that will hold water. The wells will run again, they will survive this year. They say a prayer perhaps for those who did not last long enough to be able to say this.

In the South the fields of war are silenced by the rain. The drops clatter down like the rattle of bones in a grey mist of moving ghosts, like the echo of laughter, like the shadow of weeping.

In the offices of the government the clerks and the murrasalas *are thankful because once more the hand of God has intervened and saved them the trouble of doing anything. They sit down and order more tea.*

The man called Spiro saw the body lying face down across the raw parallel scars that carved through the earth. The big headlights from the German-built truck picked him out in the churned-up mud. The truck pulled to a halt and Spiro stared out through the night and the rain. He had thought it was a gazelle or antelope, hurt perhaps, or somebody's meal abandoned in fright. He looked carefully round through the surrounding shadows for any sign of movement, then he took the rifle from the rack behind his seat and checked it was loaded. He climbed down from the high cab, dropping the last foot or so into deep sticky mud that gripped his boots.

Keeping his rifle levelled, Spiro turned the body over with the toe of his boot. Rain splashed into the closed eyes and rolled down the face. Spiro had never seen Tanner in his life; he had no idea what he should be doing out here in the middle of the night. He saw the bandage and the wounded leg. He saw the torn ragged clothing and the bare feet. He was wondering how this man had come to be here in the middle of nowhere in the centre of a rainstorm.

Glancing carefully round in the half-light and shadows thrown by the beams of the truck's headlamps, Spiro could see nothing moving. He could hear nothing but the rumble of the diesel and the hiss of the rain. He crouched down in the mud and felt for a pulse.

When Tanner came round he was being jolted around in the back of the truck, between the cardboard boxes stacked around him. He had no idea where he was. He could remember fragments of the past few days. The walking and the rain and the pain in his leg. He could remember now the face of the man who was Spiro. How had he found him? His back hurt and the rough sacks he was lying on were wearing his skin raw. When he closed his eyes the rain on the canvas over his head sounded like a flurry of whispering voices. His leg twitched and the muscle began to cramp.

It was daylight the following morning when he woke again. The truck had stopped moving. The canvas awning was pulled aside and a figure climbed over the tailboard.

'Gilmour? Is that you?' He hardly recognised his own voice.

Spiro came nearer, holding out a bottle for Tanner to drink. The water spilt and dribbled down his chin.

'You're British?' Spiro was curious.

'Yes . . . no.'

Spiro nodded his head as though he hadn't expected an answer. He reached into his pocket for a cigarette. It was after he had lit it that he seemed to remember his manners and offered the packet. Tanner dropped the first one so Spiro lit another and placed it between his lips.

'I would ask you how you got here, and where all this blood came from,' said Spiro, indicating Tanner's clothes. 'But it's none of my business.'

'I killed a man,' said Tanner flatly. He half expected to be told that it wasn't true.

'It's none of my business, like I say.' Spiro reached down and tore at the ripped fabric to examine the wound in Tanner's leg. 'How does it feel?'

'It's not too bad. It doesn't hurt so much now.'

Spiro got to his feet. 'You need to get to a doctor. It's probably best if I take you to a place not far from here. The priest there can take care of you.' He started towards the back of the truck. He stopped and opened one of the cartons. He held out a bottle, twisting off the cap. Tanner took the bottle marked 'Molotte Finest Gin'.

'If the pain gets worse. It's all I've got.' he said apologetically before dropping out of sight over the back of the truck. A few minutes later the engine started and they moved off.

Father Joseph was originally a member of the Ayuot Dinka tribe. He had changed his name when he was converted to Catholicism. He pushed his way through the gathered crowd of gawping children and bored women. Behind him two older boys of around fifteen carried a wooden bed between them. Father Joseph reached the centre of the gathering where Spiro stood holding up the bloodstained ragged figure of a young man. The boys carrying the bed turned neatly to line themselves up alongside and Spiro lowered Tanner on to the bedstrings. Spiro and Father Joseph walked back to the mission house together.

'Who is he that you have brought to us?'

'I don't know, Father. I found him in the road last night.'

'He has been hurt in a battle somewhere,' mused Father Joseph.

'I couldn't tell you anything about that, Father,' replied Spiro.

'Of course not.'

Tanner was placed in a small green room with bare walls and only very sparse furniture: a chair by the bed, a tin cornet with a plastic rose fixed to the wall, a wooden crucifix over the bed. A naked lightbulb hanging from the ceiling glared straight into Tanner's eyes. Father Joseph dressed Tanner's wound as best he could.

'You have lost a lot of blood and I fear that there is some infection,' he announced when he had finished. There were no drugs or antibiotics at the mission apart from simple antiseptics.

'You are too sick to be moved but I have sent a boy for a doctor.' Joseph wiped his hands with a towel and moved to pull the window shutters closed.

'You must try to rest for the time being. It will take a day or so, that is all.'

179

Tanner felt almost too weak to talk but he felt the need to ask; 'How did I get here?' There was no one who could answer him. And so finally he was alone. The room seemed to beat softly, turning gently in its slumber. He drifted back and forth from the clutch of dreams that threatened to engulf him. A jumbled splice of his past accelerated and juxtaposed in a kind of cross reference. He appeared to have reached the temporary haven of a watershed where suddenly he could no longer feel time rushing past him. The turmoil of the last weeks had finally abated, it seemed, and there was a moment of silence. He was wondering where exactly his journey had begun, where the seed had been planted in him that had eventually led him to this time and place.

The room was permeated with that sense of reverence which he associated with the crucifix hanging on the wall opposite. The memory of the sweep of starched cotton as the Priest left the room. There was something final about this room.

He realised that he had never really thought about death before.

Of course he had in the way that most people might. In the abstract manner that conceals the menace of terminal illness and fatal accident. He had thought of death only in terms of something quite detached from the daily processes by which monotony leads to impenetrable immunity.

So how had he come to reach this final time and place? Was it simply a matter of fate or had he finally achieved that which he had always been seeking, albeit unconciously? His death in this place seemed now assured. The Priest's assistant, the Sister, had scuffed through the freshly swept room muttering to herself in a language Tanner could not recognise. He could see it in her eyes, which never rested on his for more than a hasty curious moment before they were jerked away. He could smell it in the dust of the freshly swept room that preserved the odour of the inevitable amnesia that would erase the memory of him after he was gone. He could feel it in the poison that seeped through his body from the septic wound in his leg. The trace of poison placed there in the struggle with Gilmour.

And what of Gilmour?

If he was to die here in this room now for having tried to stop

180

Gilmour, would he not rather have changed things if he could? To save his own life? Had he known, would he not have taken a different course of action? Of course this made no sense. He could not undo what he had done, but it made him think about why exactly he had killed Gilmour. He had finally reached the challenge of his journey, of his lifetime, in that night with Gilmour. He had acted finally and in doing so he had killed a man, but he had also released himself from the years of frustration and lack of direction. He had seen in an instant what he had to do and he had carried it out.

He closed his eyes and the image of Gilmour flooded into his mind. The dead man ripped to shreds by the talons and hooked beaks of the birds. He tried to make the swollen river wash the body away but it wouldn't go.

The door opened a crack and the Sister peered through at him.

They were waiting for him to die. Her small round face disappeared and the door closed. The affair had an almost farcical side to it. This moment of gravity, his final hours, was being turned into a hysterical drama, a black comedy in which the only person who would not walk out of the theatre wiping the tears of laughter from his eyes would be the main character: himself.

It seemed so long ago that he had first set out to find this country. He thought about the part of his life that he had spent here. About the journey that had commenced with his meeting Gilmour for the first time, at the hotel. He could remember the precise feeling of coming into the air-conditioned lobby. He thought about how everything had led to his conflict with Gilmour. He had come here looking for a place to live, to rest and of perhaps even to die. How could he question that he had ended up in this room, this particular room for his sins?

They were waiting for him to die.

When he was done there would be no sign of his passing but the empty bed which the curious Sister would tidy up in her obsessive manner. He wondered if anyone would find out about his death. The company would presume him lost, but there would be nothing they could do about it. Who would inform his mother, or his father? And Nina, she might never find out. Perhaps she would

181

go through life wondering from time to time what had become of him. She might even address a letter to him and be disappointed when she did not receive a reply.

He did not want to die so soon.

There had not been enough time, and he had wasted so much of what there had been. It was clear to him now that there had been reason in his movement. The only truth he had found was in motion: a kinetic sense of stability. Was it motion that brought stability or the need for stability that led him to keep moving?

The Priest never answered any of his questions truthfully. When he asked him about his leg he was told that it was getting better, though he knew himself that it was getting worse. When he asked about the doctor and when he might be arriving the Priest had told him that they were expecting him at any minute. But from the sound of the rain he knew that no one was moving anywhere in this weather, all the roads would have been washed out.

He was no longer awake for continuous periods of time. He found himself instead sinking into a state of semi-consciousness. The sunlight through the rain drew patterns on the wall. Colours flooded across the ceiling – sapphire, gold and viridian. Smoke and acrid fragments whined past his ears. He felt himself falling.

He was back on the river. It was a warm, cloudless day, listless. The old dugout canoe drifted across the shimmer of water casting a net of fingerprint ripples from the prow of the craft. There was a hawk wrestling with its catch. He saw the fish come free and fall slowly from that great height to vanish back into the water, breaking the glass surface as it disappeared. In his hands there was a compass, whose needle seemed to swing from pole to pole, spinning like a top. He closed his eyes and fell asleep in the sun. When he woke the canoe had just nudged the side of the paddleboat. It seemed to have been brought up from the bottom of the river covered in long strands of grass and reeds. Water poured from the broken windows and doorways. He grasped the railing and tried to pull himself on to the deck but he couldn't. When he looked down he realised that his leg was missing. He heard a

182

sound and looked up to see Gilmour standing in the shade of the upper deck. His skull was caved in and blood poured from his head and nose, from behind his eyes. He stood looking at Tanner. There was a sudden clatter of running feet and a small spotted jackal rushed out from the debris of the cabins and splashed into the water alongside the canoe. Startled, Tanner let go his grip and he began to drift away again. He glimpsed the ugly head bobbing up and down as it swam away, then he was gone. He fell into the back of the canoe and the current swept him away. Barefoot children scampered naked along the flat river bank. They called out and waved their arms. He couldn't hear what they were saying but they seemed to be laughing, smiling. They pointed down the river. He shook his head at them to indicate that he didn't understand and then he was gone.

He felt himself begin to come awake, very slowly as though he were being drawn all the time, deeper into sleep. The Priest was holding on to his arm, leaning over him. Over his shoulder he could see the old crow of a Sister hanging back by the door.

'Is there anything you feel the need to confess?' asked Father Joseph.

'No, I don't think so,' replied Tanner. His voice seemed a long way off.

Father Joseph drew a breath and a look of anxiety crossed his face. 'Do not be concerned. If your conscience is good then God will receive you.' He hesitated awkwardly. 'You do believe in God?'

'Which god?'

The faces receded and the voices dissolved. He held his hand up to his face and he could see the lines drawn there. The confusion of lines and strokes seemed to resemble a map. He could feel the pattern in his fingertips and he heard the sound of the rain that was too late. He wanted to know that his part had not gone unnoticed. That his journey had served some kind of purpose, but of course such gratitude is rare in life.

He saw the swirling muddy rivers, the empty villages and the dead and wounded. He saw the homeless and the nomads who had nowhere to go and he realised that such things had happened before and would come again, but those who survived would return. The rains which they waited for would one day come. He sank further into his vision until finally it took precedence over his life; he lost sight of reality and in that instant he was gone.

Tanner, or the one known by that name, passed away in a quiet moment, somewhere between the drops of rain that fell like a wave, like a heartbeat, on the tin roof of the mission.